The Distancer

Jake Alexander Raines

For my wife, Raven.
This book would not exist without her.

1

It's difficult to remember which year I traveled back from. Was it 2080 or 2075 or maybe 2070? I don't know. The Time Keeper on my Continuum Resetter broke when I went back. That's ironic, considering the purpose of the design is to send you back. Or forward. My guess is that CyberSynth designed it that way so if someone outside of the organization ever had the opportunity to break the code and use it the way the Enlisters did, you wouldn't be able to figure out where you went. Or where you were going to end up when you Distanced again. I know the code well enough to count the number of years forward or backward if I have a starting point. And I do remember the year I went back to, the memories are vivid.

I saw a bird glide overhead and land on a bench in front of me. As I walked past, it studied me and that felt odd. I stopped to swat it with the back of my hand and expected it to fly off, but to my surprise, I made contact. Its life-like wings fluttered as it spiraled to the ground and began to short out. I couldn't believe what I was seeing. Either CyberSynth sent back a Black Bird Camera to track me, and that meant Enlisters were on the way, or they had invented the Black Bird Cameras long ago and everything was so much worse than I imagined. My paranoia felt heavy in my chest and I had to act fast. Instead, I froze. For several minutes, I stood there and stared at the lifeless Black Bird Camera. That's redundant, they're lifeless to begin with. As I looked on, I ran through an infinite number of scenarios.

If I do nothing, Enlisters will be here within minutes and I will be killed. CyberSynth may even send Enlisters back to before I saw the Black Bird Camera and I'll be taken out by the end of this thought. I should study it to determine if they sent it back or if it was already here. If it was here first, then they won't know I'm here. They may know I'm here and are watching to see what I do. This is a dream. This is not a dream, this is real. Pick up the bird and walk away. Why don't I jump back further? No, I came to this year for a reason. I whispered "Pick up the bird and walk away". I shoved the Black Bird Camera in my bag and continued walking. I didn't know what I was going to do with it or even where to go. My plan was to Distance and not much thought had been put into anything else.

I kept on until I found a cheap, rundown motel. A man came out from behind the desk and didn't offer much of a greeting. I told him I needed a room and he started to ask for identification. Having my name on file was not in my best interest so I offered to pay for my room for a week up front. I placed a stack of money on the desk.

"That's more than enough for a week," I said.

"You a drug dealer?" He asked as he picked up the cash.

I laughed and said, "No, just need a place to stay for a little while."

Without resisting at all, he set up a keycard and handed it to me. "Quiet hours are after 10 PM, try not to trash the room. 14 is outside the door to the right." I took the card, thanked him, and headed out.

I had given him about three to five thousand dollars. That was pretty steep but my cash flow was endless. Additive Manufacturing, also known as "3-D Printing", had become commonplace in my lifetime; the same way computers became basic appliances in the late 20th and early 21st centuries. We used to print old money for fun as children. It was authentic to whatever era we selected on our AM machines. Complete with watermarks and all of the security features, or lack thereof. The Continuum Resetter I had stolen was capable of Additive Manufacturing. And the technology had become so advanced that the refillable supplies built into the device would last for years. There was no limit to the items I could print at will.

I stuck the keycard into the slot and heard the lock click. I pushed open the door and stepped inside. It was a typical room, bed, bathroom, dresser with a TV on top, and an air conditioning unit. The air it produced was thick and cold, a luxury I had never been afforded. Sweat poured down my face as I went to the sink and held my hands under the water. I drank several handfuls then slumped down onto the floor, resting my back against the bed. I got lost looking at the pattern on the carpet and listening to the hum of the air conditioner. After everything I had done, I knew Enlisters were coming for me.

I was once a Lead Developer of the Distancing technology, and it was new when I joined the project. It was also my sole assignment for years and we had accomplished a lot in that period. We took it from a concept to a full fledged operation that worked with almost no flaws. That ride lasted until I had an opportunity to visit the Rilekrin factory, the place where the raw materials were mined and developed. That experience was unnerving and I couldn't stop thinking about the conditions the workers were subjected to. I returned to headquarters later on and shared what I saw with others on my team. People began calling the ethics of my employer into question; both from inside and outside of the company.

Supported by the government, with a reach that expanded far and wide across every facet of life, CyberSynth was everywhere. Many of us were unhappy with the Corporate-Government unification, as well as the condition of the Rilekrin factory, and because of that, subsequent employee strikes broke out. Somehow, word got back to the C-level Executives that I was the one responsible. I was stripped of my title and sent to a live-in manufacturing plant, much like Rilekrin.

The air in that factory was almost unbreathable and some days there was not enough food for everyone. People I considered friends had died. I was being threatened with death myself by the Enlisters running the factory. Those Enlisters weren't programmed to know who I was or why I was there. I kept quiet about my technical knowledge and tried not to draw any attention to myself. The Enlisters had no concept of why CyberSynth wanted me killed at worst, and sequestered in a factory, at best. The program running in the Operating Systems of the Enlisters received input and did not generate commands on its own. The Artificial Intelligence we built figured out how to spawn subprocesses to delegate the control of others to Organic Machines. These particular models were referred to as "Enlisters" because of the inherent violent tendencies present in the code running on their Operating Systems. They were used to keep order wherever they were deployed and had the authority to arrest anyone deemed an "offender", a term with an ever-changing definition. If someone destroyed an Enlister, they would be captured and killed. There was no jury trial or due process. It was considered the ultimate crime by CyberSynth, punishable by death. On the day I decided to Distance back, I killed ten Enlisters at once; the entire group assigned to our floor.

I waited until the end of the day and went to my locker to gather my things. I put on my jacket, wrapped a rag around my face, and went to the center of the pod. Most of us wore rags to combat the smell of the factory anyway and it was an effective way to obscure my face. I knew that once these commands were executed, I was going to be the most wanted man in the world. I knelt down and pretended to re-tie my boot. Using the Continuum

Resetter I had stolen when I was a Developer, I pulled up the Terminal application, exploited a flaw in the motherboards and executed very simple commands.

Admin -execute fireone /shutdown
Admin -execute invert /shutdown
Admin -execute deadloop /shutdown

Those stopped the database connections for all of the Enlisters and deleted the Admin account in their Operating System. It made rolling back the changes impossible.

After a few seconds, every Enlister dropped to the floor and vibrated, which immediately alerted the Enlisters on every level of the plant. Hell broke loose when the workers figured out what was happening. They kicked the doors, knocked over equipment, and destroyed everything in sight. An alarm blared that was loud enough to drown out even the most basic thoughts. An already tense day had boiled over into actual violence. I ran toward my cell and prepared to travel back. I pulled up the Distancing program and waited for what felt like hours. Once I entered the destination and the date, I had thirty seconds before the sequence would initiate. More Enlisters entered the first floor and a fire had broken out. Workers were screaming, some had been killed, some were bloodied on the factory floor. A number of Enlisters had been destroyed as well. The oil from their bodies formed black pools, one of which had spread to my feet. I looked down at my reflection, realizing that I could become the catalyst for an undoing of a corrupt world long past its expiration. Or, I wouldn't survive long enough to be anything other than a man who got apprehended, tortured, then burned in a pile with other offenders.

With ten seconds left in the countdown, an Enlister ran into my cell and grabbed me by the neck with its cold hand. It ripped off the rag and scanned my face. "Jonas Branford, you are hereby under detainment under the authority of CyberSynth Incorporated for the crimes you have committed against CyberSynth Incorporated. Please place your hands behind your back."

It looked down at the Continuum Resetter and knew right away what was happening. "We will find you, Jonas Branford. There is no escape."

As soon as the last word exited its mouth, I saw a bright flash of light and heard nothing. It was beyond silent, like being under water. The light grew brighter, sound returned, and I found myself on a street corner in 2026.

2

My eyes shot open in the middle of the night. I never checked the room for bugs or anything else CyberSynth could use for reconnaissance on my whereabouts. I had fallen asleep on the floor by mistake. I ripped open every drawer, flipped over the mattress, I tore the room apart but couldn't find anything. Out of breath, I sat back down on the floor. I ripped the cord on the alarm clock out of the wall by mistake so I had no idea of the time. It was very late and I knew that I would not get much accomplished before sunrise so I decided to rest until morning.

When I awoke, I rushed to the bathroom and drank from the sink again. The water tasted cleaner than it did before. Where I came from, water was contaminated and had to be boiled for hours before it could be consumed. Some parts of the world had begun wars over water and it was the last resource not out-right owned by a corporation. Africa and even some parts of America became desolate wastelands due to the lack of available water for the population. That seemed to work in CyberSynth's favor when it came to controlling the populace, though it was not part of their original plan. People in the 21st century didn't know how fortunate it was to have clean drinking water at their disposal, and that is why, I think, complacency set in when artificial intelligence took over. It made a simple life even easier so why put up a fight? There didn't seem to be any downside, in the beginning. And at the pace that things changed, it was a gradual takeover as people handed over day-to-day tasks to Organic Machines; rather than an immediate shift in society. At the advent, it was all text-based interactions that required human input. Then, it expanded into the arts, sciences, sales, and call centers. It was only a matter of time before what once hidden behind a screen made the jump into a physical body standing right in front of you.

I laid on the bed and stared at the ceiling as light came through the curtains. I knew how CyberSynth formed and I had a short list of important people that I was searching for, but that was all I had. The people behind the formation of the company were entrepreneurs that had acquired wealth and status through their own careers. At some point, the technologies of each of their companies presented an opportunity for them to merge into a new corporation. The first technology developed was called the "Micro Organic Robotic System" or MORS. The MORS were administered through injections and were capable of rapid learning and self-reproduction. The MORS was also designed to work day and night to repair the host's internal organs. And as those organs are repaired, the body is replaced by the MORS and anyone with these injections becomes less human. Except for the mind, Artificial intelligence never achieved consciousness. However, CyberSynth developed a way to merge the body with machines at an organic level. So while artificial intelligence does not have consciousness, people who inject MORS have the power of machines, with real, human functions. The leaders of the company, the people who were also responsible for the establishment of the corporation, wanted to live free from disease and death, with ultimate control over humanity. And I made it my goal to eliminate every one of them. Even if I had to die.

I left my room to search for a vehicle. As I was leaving, a different clerk approached from out of an empty room and startled me. I almost threw her to the ground and ran.

"You're staying in 14, right?"

"Yeah, that's right." I said, as my heart thumped in my chest.

"Someone was here looking for you a little while ago."

My mouth dried up as I fought the next words off of my tongue.

"Did they leave a name?" I asked.

"No sir, he didn't say much but he asked if you were staying here. I told him that you didn't mention you were expecting a guest so we couldn't give him your room number."

She walked toward the lobby and I followed beside her. I said the person must have been mistaken as I was here on business and didn't know anyone in town. I had to check out and find another place to stay. My mission would be short lived if I didn't get work as fast as possible. How did the Enlisters know where I was? How did I know that woman wasn't an Enlister herself?

Since I could print cash at will, it felt like a better idea to purchase a vehicle instead of trying to steal one. Keeping crime to a minimum would be the best way for me to keep the eyes of the law off of me. I was in a centralized location and I had a map of the area loaded onto my Continuum Resetter. I went into a shaded alleyway and studied the map. I found a used car dealership two miles away, wrote the directions on my arm and put my

Continuum Resetter back in my bag. I started to walk off when I stopped myself. Running commands to shutdown an is Enlister something I was capable, of but that wouldn't work without planning ahead. If I got ambushed, I would need a weapon. I pulled the map back up, searched for a gun store, and found one even closer than the car dealership. It happened to be next to a military surplus store. I wrote some additional notes on my arm and left the alleyway. As soon as the sunlight hit my face, I felt a hand on my shoulder and heard a deep, lifeless voice.

"Jonas Branford, stop where you are."

I threw my elbow back and hit the Enlister in the mouth. It stumbled, looked up and charged at me, oil spilling from its teeth. I dodged back into the alleyway and grabbed a brick off of the ground. Before I could hit it again, it grabbed me by the throat, right beneath my jaw, and lifted me off the ground.

"We know what you are doing here, Jonas, and we cannot let you do that."

I shut my eyes and pretended to pass out. The Enlister laid me on my stomach and tried to restrain my hands behind my back. I gasped for air and kicked it at the knees. I heard a loud snap as I rolled onto my back. Its eyes flashed red and white as it collapsed. I took the brick and slammed it right into the Enlisters forehead. At this point, the Malfunction Sequence kicked off, and that would send a signal to other Enlisters in the area. Before that could finish, I stood over its body and yanked on the skull. I managed to pull it all the way around once. The synthetic skin ripped and the neck cracked. I pushed it around the opposite way and ripped off more skin. I stuck my hand in and pulled out as many of the components as I could, then ripped the head off its body. Oil poured out onto the ground and smoke filled the alleyway. The panic in my stomach rose to my chest. I was covered in oil and was no longer inconspicuous. My plan had now grown more difficult. I dragged the Enlister to a nearby dumpster, ripped off its shirt to wipe my face and arms, then dropped it and the skull inside. I needed new clothes. No, I needed a new plan. I needed A vehicle. I needed…

The voice in my head went quiet. As I stared off in the alleyway, I saw a light blinking to my left. I turned my head and on the ground laid a Control Baton; the Enlister must have dropped it. I picked it up and it weighed nothing. These were weapons we knew existed but had never seen. It was issued to the newest model of Enlisters and intended for the worst offenders. We always assumed it was a myth. It was made of an unknown alloy material. Ultra-lightweight, but as dense as Iron, it could cripple a 250 pound man with a minimal swing. It was like Onyx in color with a collection of lighted, asymmetrical barbs at the end, and was about a meter length. The handle was some type of rubber that allowed for shock absorption so repeated hits could be dealt in rapid succession. A small button on the side made the weapon retractable and that much more dangerous. The battery had an infinite charge, so the lights never faded. Enlisters didn't have souls but this weapon made them feel invincible.

While my plan was broken or at the very least, under repair, the Control Baton gave me an advantage over the machines coming after me. Or a chance to die with dignity. It also meant that CyberSynth were sending back later model Enlisters that were stronger and faster than the ones I had faced before. Each one equipped with the same weapon. I put the Control Baton into my bag and pulled out the Black Bird Camera. I looked at it again and examined the mechanical parts that hung from its side. It looked so real from afar and even more realistic up close. The amount of detail in the feathers down to the feet was impressive. There was no difference in appearance from theses and the real birds you would see on the street. I started to put it back into my bag when its head tilted and its eyes began to blink. It must have still had an active signal, which is how the Enlisters were able to find me. Out of reflex, I threw it onto the ground and smashed it into pieces. I was jumpy and needed to get out of there.

I continued towards the destination I had sprawled on my arm that was now smeared and illegible thanks to the oil from the Enlister. On my way, I found a thrift store and went inside. I still needed to change out of my factory clothes and into something that would allow me to blend in. I bought a black t-shirt and black jeans. The darker the clothes, the better. I paid for everything, changed in the bathroom, and left the thrift store. Once I pushed open the door and stepped onto the pavement, I saw an armed robbery taking place at a convenience store across the street.

There were two men with handguns standing in the front of the store, and a car parked outside. I could hear the engine running from where I was so it was a perfect opportunity for me to get a vehicle. I reached into my bag, pulled out the Control Baton and jogged across the street. As I approached the store, the two men exited the store.

I shouted at them, "Excuse me!" and I hit one of them in the chest with the Control Baton. He flew back and into the outside wall.

His accomplice yelled, "Whoa, what the fuck?!" and tried to point his gun at me. I hit him in the hand and destroyed most of his fingers. He dropped his gun and fell to the ground, screaming. I picked the gun, got into their car, and drove off.

I turned my head to get out of the parking lot and saw a semiautomatic rifle laying across the back seat. That was an unexpected but welcomed surprise.

Now, I needed a place to stop so I could print new plates and tags to avoid what would be an insurmountable task of evading the police. Not only was this vehicle stolen, it had been used to commit a crime so changing out that out was a top priority. I needed ammo, too. The AM Machine function was great for printing out most things but I couldn't print guns, bullets, or explosives so I located a gun store on my Continuum Resetter and made that my new destination.

3

The glare on the front windows, along with the tint made it very hard to tell if anyone was inside of the Guns & Ammo Depot. The blacktop was hot under my feet as I went up to the door. I guess some things about Texas hadn't changed in all of the decades that had passed up until I was born. The Rilekrin factory was a small piece of Hell, thanks in large part to the heat we experienced in the summer months.

Right away, I felt the cold rush of air as soon as I walked inside. A long glass case filled with handguns and knives was on the right and a section for tactical gear on the left. Mannequins with ballistic vests were scattered throughout the store.

"Can I help you find something?" asked a tall, older man standing behind the glass case.

"Yeah, I'm looking for 9 mm FMJ."

He paused and asked "How many boxes do you need?"

That question had not even crossed my mind. How much ammo did I need? What type of rifle was in the back seat? I needed ammo for that too. I know the handgun was a 9mm but what about the rifle? I couldn't just bring it inside and ask him. Some rifles use .223 caliber. How much ammo did I need?!

"How many per box?" I asked, wondering if I had taken too long to answer.

"Well, we have boxes of 50, 100 and 500. I can do two boxes of 500 for $100. They're $65 each, by themselves."

"OK, I can do that."

He grabbed two boxes and set them down on the counter. The words "Eskew 9mm 115-Grain FMJ Bullets 500 Count" were written across the front.

"Is there anything else I can get you?"

"Yeah, let's do some .223s as well."

"We got boxes of 200 for $120. How many rounds are you looking for?"

"I'll take a thousand of those as well."

He placed five more boxes of Eskew ammo down on the counter.

"Is that gonna be it for today?"

"Yeah, that's it."

"OK, so two boxes of 500 for $100, 5 boxes of 200 for $120, each. That comes out to $700."

I took out seven one hundred dollar bills and handed them over. He put the money in his register and the boxes into a black bag. I thanked him and went back out to my car.

I didn't know very much about firearms but I had some experience from back in my teens. My friend's father was ex-military and he used to take us out to abandoned neighborhoods to shoot at dilapidated houses. It had been a few decades so I was hoping the muscle memory would kick in when it was time to pull the trigger.

I opened the trunk and found two magazines for the rifle that were already loaded with .223s. I put those next to the rifle in the backseat, shoved the empty 9mm magazine into my pocket, and left the boxes of ammo in the trunk.

I also found a small tool box with a screwdriver among some other tools. The plates needed to be changed so I pulled up the program on the Continuum Resetter and got to work. I searched for a car that matched the description of the one I was driving. I found an almost identical match in the database for a call that had been totaled.

The printing capability of my Continuum Resetter was my saving grace and an integral part of my decision to travel back to 2026. Where I came from, the Government had decided to cut down on spending and laid off thousands of people. They implemented a system that required us to rely on AM Machines to do most of the work that was once the responsibility of the Department of Motor Vehicles and the Department of Public Safety. Regular people printed new license plates and tags on their own. AM Machines would talk to various State and Federal agencies and we would print what was required on an as needed basis. The information available to consumers would also go as far back as 150 years to allow for classic cars to stay up to date; so I knew chances were high I could find a vehicle with no issues. And with any technology, criminals exploited backdoors in the software and people were able to steal cars and print plates at will with little chance of being caught. All you had to do was modify the Automotive software on the AM Machine to allow full access.

I replaced the plate on the rear then the plate and tag on the front. I walked to a dumpster to throw away the old plates and stopped as soon as I turned back around. There were at least fifty Black Bird Cameras on the roof of the gun store, on the power lines, and on the trunk of my car. All of them blinking and turning their heads in different directions, gathering as much data as possible. I had never seen so many at once in all of my life. The transmissions between the Black Bird Cameras and the Enlisters had to have been taking place in real-time and I expected more Enlisters to show up at any moment. With one swing of the Control Baton, I knocked the Black Bird Cameras off of the trunk. The others flew away as I yanked the door open and turned the ignition. I threw the car into drive and pressed my foot on the gas. The tires screeched as I sped away from the gun store, unsure of where to go next.

4

   The first on my target list was Donovan
White. He was the Chief Architect of the MORS
technology and CEO of Red Index, one of the three
companies that would later merge to become
CyberSynth. I didn't have a lot of information on
him, or any of the targets for that matter. The
merger of the three companies, with backing from a
single investor took place in 2026; and the CEO of
each company along with the investor knew each
other on a professional level. I planned to exploit
any information Donovan had about his colleagues
and use it to my advantage. I found the address of
the Red Index headquarters using my Continuum
Resetter and headed across the city.

   Donovan was still alive in the year I came
from, all of the people I wanted to kill were still
alive, thanks to their technology. These people had
devised a way to live beyond their normal lifespan,
enslave the public, and fuse with the US
Government along the way. The atrocities
CyberSynth was guilty of were close to infinite in
number. The details of that tend to bore me since I
had been born during and spent most of my adult
life living through it. While I didn't seek sympathy
from anyone, I will say that my life was nothing

short of terrible. You were either wealthy and lived in the Purified Domes or you were poor. There is no other way to explain the divide. The coveted Middle Class that we learned about in school that had disappeared in the 2050's was less than a shell of itself when I was born. My job as a Programmer wasn't as glamorous as it might sound. My position had been devalued due to humanity's utilization of Artificial Intelligence and my eventual placement in the Rilekrin plant was inevitable. I would have ended up there regardless of speaking out against my company, due to the shift in the need for human Programmers.

CyberSynth had created an entire workforce made up of Enlisters who performed most of the jobs assumed by humans in the past. Average people became more than secondary to the elitist class. Our air wasn't even clean enough to breathe, our water was dirty, our jobs were awful, and we were relegated to the most concrete areas of all the major cities. We had nowhere to grow vegetation and we were starved of our most basic resources in some areas. CyberSynth had become more powerful than any Government in the world. So much so that our own Government had blurred the lines between the two. CyberSynth had not only infiltrated the Government, they owned it. Calling my world a "dystopia" had some comfort to it since it was at least a label. There was no word to describe our way of life. Humanity was a subordinate of its own creation. What was once considered an advancement in technology was now the bearer of ruin.

After months of research, I figured out there were four people who were viewed as the brain trust of CyberSynth: Donovan White, former CEO of Red Index and inventor of the MORS technology. Renata Caldwell, former CEO of the anti-aging research firm Fountain Research Partners. Ellis Murdoch, the inventor of Organic Machine technology and founder and CEO of BionicShift. And Xavier Lambert, entrepreneur and owner of multiple businesses; most notable, was a private Military operation known to the public as StarBurner Services.

StarBurner meddled in foreign and domestic relations for multiple world governments. They supplied weapons to the enemies of various nations, then offered mercenary services in return. They burnt the war machine candle at both ends and saw profits hit almost one billion dollars three years after his company was founded. All of the people I wanted dead were evil, but Xavier was the Devil's Son. He once called in a Drone Strike to a wedding in Dubai because the person who sold the bride and groom the cake owed the Mexican Drug Cartels millions of dollars. He would take money from anyone for anything with no care for morals or ethics. He was ruthless to say the least and was the main driver behind the success of CyberSynth as its primary investor. Being affiliated with the military and the US Government gave Xavier a very good idea of the lay of the land as far as emerging technologies were concerned. He knew what was being developed well before the public. And when the pieces were in place, he put in offers to purchase the three companies and merged them into one. Xavier was the main and most difficult target. He was well trained and always traveled with trusted "Security Advisers", which was a euphemism for bodyguards. Getting to him was difficult and I needed to take out Renata, Donovan and Ellis first. I was afraid that if I killed Xavier before I got to others, everyone would go into seclusion and it would be impossible to locate them all. And each of them did deserve to die.

Renata Caldwell was party to a lawsuit involving illegal experimentations on inner city youth for beauty products. She had her agency lure vulnerable young women and promise them cash payments for testing out unreleased skin care products. Most of the women had been left infertile, and others died from reactions to the chemicals Renata's company had used. She was found guilty of Conspiracy to Conceal and Cover Up but was only punished with probation and ordered to pay a fine. When asked by reporters about this offense, she joked and referred to "population control". In addition to lawsuits, Renata was known for owning sweatshops and employing children in other countries. She was as ruthless and relentless in the world of Beauty Supply as Xavier was as a mercenary. People referred to her as the "Mother of Death".

Ellis Murdoch and Donovan White had similar backgrounds. Both were born into wealth and both were young CEO's that had created new technologies that made them millionaires. Ellis was known for competition buy-outs where he would purchase a company and lay off the entire staff. He did this again and again until all rival companies were eliminated. It was a self-made monopoly and the Government did nothing to stop it from happening. He participated in rounds of layoffs as CEO of BionicShift as well and replaced the staff with Organic Machines in the 2020's. He once said that the "return on investment when you replace a person with an Organic Machine is almost immediate considering you don't have to listen to their opinions any longer."

Donovan had fired dozens of his employees as well, before and after the merger that created CyberSynth. Many of his former employers attempted to take him to court over wrongful termination and harassment scandals, but each of them died under mysterious circumstances before the trials began. He earned the nickname "Date Rape Donovan" and his company paid off women that he had been accused of raping. He had an affinity for younger women and frequented strip clubs and whore houses. I didn't know a lot about either of them prior to the start of their careers and it was as if they had appeared one day out of nothing, loaded with endless amounts of money. Donovan and Ellis were scumbags and were also soft targets. Their arrogance would get in the way, maybe *my* arrogance would get in the way.

I should stop and think: I've never killed anyone before, what makes me think I could kill any of these people? What happens to me if I do kill one of them? I expect that something in this present will change. Will I alter the future so much so that I won't even recognize myself in the mirror? What made me think I was capable of anything other than failing? I had never felt fulfilled up until this point, what made this any different? How will killing someone alter the future?! What is going to happen to me?!

I stopped myself. None of those points mattered. I knew I would bleed and I expected to die. That was my advantage over the enemy, I accepted death while CyberSynth tried to defy it. My life was expendable and it held little value in my own eyes. That was ironic, considering I was going to sacrifice myself to save countless people; some of whom weren't even alive yet. I hadn't considered what would happen once the first person was off my list. I guess I didn't care. Whatever I could do to disrupt the flow of events in the future was considered a victory. I was angry at the way my life had unfolded, angry over the death of my parents, angry that humanity was on the brink of being wiped out. No one had anything to live for where I came from so I might as well die for something.

I glanced down at the Continuum Resetter and saw that I was nearing the Red Index headquarters. I pulled up to a stop light a block away and saw a man in a suit staring at me from the opposite corner. I stared back at him, my gun rested on my lap under my hand. Once the light turned green, I took a left and continued down the street. The man followed me with his eyes and walked a bit as I drove away. There's no way an Enlister would hesitate like that, unless that was part of their directive. Gather intelligence on my location and do not engage. Follow me and attack when it's unexpected. Or he wasn't an Enlister and it was my paranoia. I couldn't differentiate an Enlister from a normal person so I took the cautious approach and assumed everyone around me was an Enlister.

I knew from my research that Donovan drove a two-door sports car with a license plate that read "RDINDX C30". I circled through the garage and looked for Donovan's vehicle. After a handful of minutes, I found it on the third level. My nerves were on vibrate and I needed to calm down and focus. I parked my car far enough away from his so that he wouldn't notice, but close enough so that I wouldn't lose him when he drove off. It was nearing 5 PM and people were leaving for the day. I had seen Donovan in the news throughout my life. I knew what he looked like, even if he was ordinary. He stuck out with his affluence, but he was an otherwise generic looking man. I didn't doubt that I would recognize him. How I would kill him was a different story. My plan was to follow him home. Making any more of a scene in public than I already had would jeopardize my entire mission. Donovan had to die, though without any witnesses. I checked the clock. I kept my hand rested on the gear shift and let my foot off of the break.

I'm suspicious.

No, I'm not. I'm fine.

Not a single person saw that I was even in my car, each of them walked by, phones in hand. Some of them typing, some of them reading, none of them paying attention.

Donovan walked over, talking on his phone, and got into the car.

"Yeah, we're going to a happy hour, gonna be a lot of women, most of them looking for something, you know what I mean?!" His laughter echoed throughout the parking garage. A happy hour meant he wouldn't be going home right away. And that meant I would have to follow him there, to the most public place imaginable. My grip on the steering wheel tightened. I threw my car in reverse and hit the gas. I wasn't happy with it but I had to be patient, I had already come this far. A couple more hours would not make much of a difference.

We drove for thirty minutes and stopped at an upscale bar in a nicer part of the downtown district. Donovan gave his keys to a valet and I watched from the street as he walked into the bar. I figured my attire would be an issue so I printed around fifty one hundred dollar bills and stuck them into my pocket. I also didn't want to take my handgun so I left that in the trunk along with the Continuum Resetter, and tucked the Control Baton into my pocket. I locked my car and walked across the street to Free Spirits, the words flashed in neon blue lights above the door. Frosted glass, slabs of granite dawned the exterior of the entryway. A man not that much younger than me put his hand up.

"Hey man, we have a strict dress code,"

I cut him off right away. "OK, how much money do you want? How's $500?"

He was caught off guard but I had his attention. "Sir, we aren't supposed to let people in who don't meet our dress code."

"Alright, man. I'll give you $1000. I just want a drink."

"There are bars across the street…"

"$2000" I cut him off again. "Come on, man, two grand to let some asshole in who looks like he doesn't belong. Who cares? It's a weekday!"

He looked at my hands as I pulled out the stack of one hundred dollar bills and counted to 20. "Here,

$2000, I'm going inside". I stuck it in his chest and pushed him out of my way.

I strolled up to the bar and scanned the room. I saw Donovan in a booth with a couple of other people. Each of them looked like the silver spoons handed to them at birth were still in their pockets. I decided to order a drink. I was stressed out beyond belief and I was no stranger to alcohol. I didn't need liquid courage but I knew it would help ease some of the tension. A bartender approached me and asked if I needed anything.

"Two shots of whiskey and a beer, please." She nodded her head and prepared the drinks. "You know we have a dress code right?"

"Yeah, I am underdressed." I took both shots one after the other. "You're right about that."

I set down two twenty dollar bills and took my beer. There must have been a hundred people in this bar. If I took Donovan out here, it would be messy for obvious reasons and I was hoping it wouldn't come to that. Even if I had to wait for hours, I could still follow him… somewhere.

I managed to find an empty table and sat down facing the front entrance. I could see through the front windows that several birds had gathered on the power lines. I couldn't help but assume it was another flock of Black Bird Cameras. It was near dusk and the crowd continued to grow. After a while, I offered my table to a small group of people. Night had fallen and there were dozens more patrons than before. I decided to go stand at the bar, keeping my eyes on Donovan.

The bartender asked, "Do you want another round?"

"Sure, I'll take another beer."

She held up her hand and said "Five." I put down another twenty and waved for her to keep the change. I saw that Donovan was on the move but he hadn't left yet. Instead he walked toward the bathroom. I thought to follow him but decided to keep waiting. A public assassination would not help my cause. It was late, and although the bar was packed, Donovan was getting weary. This woman he had been talking to all night had left with her friends and not Donovan. I was grateful for that because I didn't want anyone else along for the ride when I blew his head off.

He downed one more shot. It looked like he was going to leave but another friend came over. He stayed for another twenty minutes, talking with this guy and also trying to pick up on another woman in his vicinity. She wasn't having any of it either and left. Donovan's friend shook his hand and also headed for the exit. The rest of his acquaintances had left and he was now alone. He grabbed his sport coat and headed for the exit as well, with me following behind him. As soon as Donovan and the exit were near, I heard two voices behind me say, in delayed unison "Hello, Jonas."

My suspicion had been confirmed. Those were Black Bird Cameras on that power line and Enlisters were here. My fear of drawing attention to myself in public, as valid as it was, no longer mattered. I could have told the two of them that I won't put up a fight, that I didn't want to see anyone get hurt.

I could have said something like "let's go outside and you can apprehend me without incident. I'm ready for this to be over". I could have done that, but I didn't. I wrapped my palm around the Control Baton, placed my thumb on the release button and prepared for the panic and chaos that would soon set in.

5

I took half a step forward and flung my right hand out of my pocket. With the Control Baton extended, I spun around and hit one of the Enlisters. It was a female model with long brown hair. Sparks spewed everywhere and her smoke emitted from her skull. She stumbled backwards, while oil covered her clothes.

"Hello, Jonas. Hello Jonas. Hello Jonas." Her voice broke up with static as she fell to the floor. People screamed and scattered. The other Enlister looked on, like he was stunned. Their design was meant to mimic human responses, that's what makes them so hard to differentiate. I moved towards the exit and shoved my way through the crowd with the Enlister not far behind me. It was absolute pandemonium. I wondered why it didn't go flying across the room like the guy outside the gas station. I guess their machine components were heavier than a human skeleton.

Donovan was now out of sight. He must have kept on before the storm erupted. I made my way out of the bar and saw another Enlister standing across the street. Our eyes met and he charged at me, full speed. Within a few steps he was slammed by a speeding truck. The truck spun out of control and crashed into a parked car, but not before the Enlister had been decapitated. More oil and more smoke. I took off running down the street, not sure where I would go. I could hear the Enlister from inside the bar close behind me. I went around a corner and another Enlister stepped out onto the street. I saw him before I got too close and stopped short. I swung around and managed to hit the Enlister from the bar in the shoulder with the Control Baton, causing his arm to malfunction. He kept after me, but it slowed him down.

The second Enlister was now on my heels, with the other trailing. The metallic footsteps pounded against the ground as it raced toward me. My car was at least three blocks away and I needed a distraction. Out of options, I ran to the nearest light post and hit the base of it with the Control Baton. This caused the transformer to explode as the post fell onto the sidewalk. Then, a blackout set in. Everything was shrouded in darkness for blocks.

I ran across the street and ducked into a drainage ditch to catch my breath. Lightning flashed, followed by thunder. I hadn't noticed how calm the air was but it became apparent when the wind picked up. Lighting flashed again, followed by thunder, and a downpour. The rain was heavy and loud. I collapsed the Control Baton, put it back into my pocket and climbed out of the ditch. I tried to familiarize myself with my surroundings but it was difficult. The Enlisters were communicating aloud with one another.

"Scanning. Negative. Scanning... Scanning... Negative. He must be gone now."

"Yes, I was processing the same response as well. We will return to his vehicle and wait."

Exterior emergency lights had kicked on at a nearby business and I could see the two of them going in opposite directions. The one with the malfunctioning arm had a bad reaction to the rain water. He changed direction, ran full speed into a concrete wall and the collision triggered an alarm. The other Enlister stopped, looked around, and continued on.

With the bar incident, the truck hitting that Enlister, the explosion and now the alarm, the police presence would increase tenfold across the half mile radius. It was imperative that I got out as fast as possible. I moved down the street again, back into the darkness, and the Enlister moved in my direction. I wasn't sure if that was a coincidence or if he was able to somehow sense my presence.

Another lightning strike lit up the night sky and the exposed metal and melted flesh around his face became apparent. The transformer pole must have clipped him somehow when it fell.

I froze.

Sirens approached from behind, I had to decide what to do. I darted across the street again, away from the drainage ditch and back toward the bar. The Enlister couldn't see me as much as I couldn't see him. As soon as I made it to the other side, lightning lit up the sky again and the Enlister walked past me, still on the street. It looked like he was heading for the police cars, which would be a disaster. There were already three destroyed Enlisters in public and now one of them was going to get into a standoff with police. I've never shot an Enlister before, but I know that unless the police went straight for the skull, there would be dead cops on top of everything else.

I stepped out onto the street, "Hey asshole! I think you're looking for me!"
Without hesitation, the Enlister ran full force in my direction. I was caught off guard but ran fast enough to keep space between us. With each step I took, everything seemed to slow down. What had unfolded was the worse case scenario. Donovan had

gotten away. CyberSynth could find me easier than I thought was possible. And emergency personnel were everywhere. It wouldn't surprise me if this was all anyone talked about for weeks or months. Across the world. Organic Machines didn't even exist yet and now three of them had been killed in plain view; four overall in one day. I continued down the street, around a corner once, then again around another corner, and stopped a block away from the bar.

The Enlister must have lost me because I couldn't see him anywhere. I looked on as the police questioned witnesses. The rain had let up some as I tried to get my bearings. I felt a hand grab the back of my neck.

"Jonas Branford, you are being taken into custody of CyberSynth, Incorporated. Remain calm."

My grip felt faint and I was losing consciousness. It had a Continuum Resetter in his hand and was entering the commands to initiate a Distance launch. I went limp and he dropped me. He lifted his shirt and detached handcuffs and feet shackles from his torso. I was on my side, and managed to get my hand around the Control Baton. He reached down to turn me over and my leg was against his foot. As he leaned down I kicked him, and grabbed his shirt with my left hand. His face landed straight onto the pavement. I got up and in one motion, released the button on the Control Baton and hit the middle of the Enlister's back. I lifted the Baton up and swung again, and hit him in the back of the head. There was nothing left but the lower half and part of the torso. You could almost feel the electricity escaping his body. The oil mixed with the rain water and started to wash down the street. I closed the Control Baton, dragged the dead Enlister to the side.

The police had both ends of the street blocked. I was a mess, my hands were covered with oil, I had cuts on my face, my clothes were drenched. Any police officer worth anything would pull me aside for questioning, without a doubt. Things were in complete disarray and the police were struggling to keep people calm. The rain had stopped and a crowd gathered. The barricade behind my car was empty and the attention was being drawn to the bright lights the local news assembled at the opposite end. I kept my head down, took out my keys, got in my car and drove around the barricade. And I kept driving, with nowhere to go. I couldn't believe Donovan got away. I had him in the parking garage. And now things were spiraling fast. I could Distance to earlier today… what if I ran into myself? That would be more disastrous than what just happened. I wasn't interested in jumping around, my goal was to go back once. Distancing was hard enough and running into my "former" self... I didn't even want to entertain that outcome.

I had to regroup. My head was killing me and I needed to sleep. The Enlisters had me beat as far as my location was concerned. There must have been more Black Birds than I could count fluttering around the city. I guess it didn't really matter where I was. CyberSynth would find me anyway. I continued on my drive through the city and saw a sign for a truck stop. I exited the highway and parked in the back. The lights around the store made it clear it was open twenty-four hours a day. That gave me a small sense of comfort. The Enlisters knew I wasn't stupid so staying in a place like this might throw them off. Or the entire staff had been replaced and soon a group of Enlisters would confront me as I slept in the back seat. I got my handgun out of the trunk, put it on the floorboard, and fell asleep.

It was brighter than I expected it to be when I woke up. How long had I slept? It must be noon. What day is it? Friday. I knew it was a Friday. The lack of fluids had gotten to me. My mouth and throat were dry and I still had a slight headache. I reached into my pocket and found some bills left over from the night before. It all seemed like a dream and played out like a nightmare. I wondered if anything made the news. I suspected that the State or Federal Governments would get involved and try to cover up as much as possible. Technology that did not exist yet had been on full display. Organic Machines themselves wouldn't exist for another ten to fifteen years and Enlisters were decades away as well. I'm sure people were asking questions.

I picked my gun up off of the floorboard, stuck it in my waistband, stumbled into the truck stop and straight for the bottled water. I opened the refrigerator door and drank two bottles back to back. I felt the eyes of the clerk watching me. The store was well cared for and she didn't like seeing a man like me, in dirty clothes, spill water on the floor as it poured off of his cheeks. Before I finished the second bottle, I pulled a twenty out of my pocket.

"Sorry", I wiped my mouth with the back of my hand, "I'm thirsty". I said as I walked up to the clerk. I handed her the money and told her to keep the change.

She didn't respond.

"Where is your restroom?" I asked.

She pointed to the back of the store and her eyes continued to follow me until I was out of sight.

I leaned into the door and it swung open. Several flies hung in the air as I walked to the sink. I washed my face to try and wipe away some of the hangover. I looked terrible and felt awful. I came up from the faucet and the flies buzzed around my head. I managed to knock one of them out of the air. It sputtered and hit the tile with a clang. I picked it up and held it close. It was dense and somewhat heavy, like a small marble. I pulled its head off and exposed wires underneath. I hit the other flies and they fell to the floor in the same way. A chill overtook my back and my hands started to sweat. CyberSynth knows I'm in this truck stop, they have surveillance all over the city. I'd never heard of anything like these flies before. And there could be additional technologies that I was not aware of. I felt outmatched but I brushed that idea to the side and put my hand on my gun. I pushed open the bathroom door and tried to act as casual as possible.

The store was dead quiet and empty, except for the clerk who was still watching me, step for step. I kept focused on the exit and moved through the aisles.

I heard the clerk's voice pierce through "Don't forget your change, Jonas."

I pulled my gun out and pointed it straight at her forehead. "How do you know my name?! Who have you been talking to?!"

She stammered with her hands up, "Hey, calm down, that guy out there paid me to say that to you."

I lowered my gun and asked "What guy?"

"The guy getting into that SUV", she said.

A man in a suit got into the back seat of an SUV.

"Did he say who he was?"

"No, he asked me if I talked to you. I told him you gave me a twenty for two bottles of water and that was it. He gave me fifty dollars to say something to you so that's all I could think of." She said, her voice cracked.

"Did he tell you my name?"

"Yeah, he said your name was Jonas. He didn't say anything else though."

I put my gun down and watched the SUV drive away.

Was that the same man outside of Donovan's office? That guy was too far away for me to make out any of his features. And I didn't know for sure if it was even the same person. Was this guy with the government? How did he know who I was? Was that Xavier Lambert? Something was off and I couldn't figure it out. Paranoia is all consuming and my focus was lost. My eyes darted across the store, over to the bathroom, then the front door, and back to the cashier. She was crying and begged me not to kill her.

"Uhh, s-sorry for that. " I saw a TV hanging above the register with my body on the screen. Another employee came in from a side door. He looked at his coworker with fear in his eyes. I didn't say anything else and bolted back to my car.

It must have been ninety-five degrees and it was so humid you could tap the air with your fingers. The clock read 4:15 PM and I couldn't believe I'd slept for over twelve hours at a truck stop. If CyberSynth wanted me dead, I wouldn't be here right now. Or I was elusive enough to stave off confrontation for just a little while. Either way, I was going back to Donovan's office and he wouldn't be making it home.

I found his car again and parked five or six spots away. As I waited, I heard his voice carry through the parking garage. He was on the phone again. I got out, gun in hand. I listened to him go on and on about the night before, telling one lie after another to whomever was on the other end.

"Yeah, she was hot, man. We went to my condo last night, but I sent her home this-" I fired two shots into the back of his head.

He was so busy rambling on that he didn't even see me there. I stepped behind him and pulled the trigger without even hesitating. His body dropped to the ground. Followed by smoke. His voice died out as he repeated the last thing he said to the person on the other end of his Blue Tooth ear piece, except it was out of sequence.

"Home sent her but I this. Home this sent her but I. But I home. Sent her…" I picked up his phone and hung it up. So many things had happened up to that point that I almost expected this. Of course Donovan was an Organic Machine. Of course there were Drone insects, of course there were people that followed me all around the city. And those "people" could be fake too. For all I knew, the sky was a hologram. The one positive in all of this is that it was oil filling the parking garage from where Donovan's body lay and not blood.

That would further confuse everyone and I doubted the local news crews would be showing up to film a dead robotic man; as much as that would be the story of the millennium. I didn't know what else to expect or how things would continue to unfold and I didn't care. Ellis Murdoch was next on my list and the day wasn't getting any longer.

6

Donvan's phone had a lot of useful information, like Ellis' address and phone number. It had emails regarding the planned merger, from Renata Caldwell and Xavier Lambert, and their addresses as well. I logged all the necessary information in my Continuum Resetter and threw the phone out of the window on the highway. My idea to storm in and kill everyone may not work in my favor. I needed to get as much information out of Ellis as possible. Was he also a machine like Donovan? Were Renata Caldwell and Xavier Lambert machines too? CyberSynth had to have a means of communication with people or Organic Machines in the present. I supposed Ellis might know something. Distancing was one thing, but sending communications to the past would be another level of technology. The Black Birds and insect Drones were not the sole means of tracking me down; it had to have gone deeper than that. Someone or something had a beat on me. Why didn't someone try to stop me from leaving the truck stop? So many questions, and very few answers.

I dug through Donovan's phone and learned that Ellis had been out of town but he would return home this evening. And there were no acknowledgements in his emails or otherwise that Donovan was an Organic Machine. Either the leaders of these companies didn't know, or it was a well kept secret. The artificial intelligence design did allow for the Organic Machines to assume the roles that most humans would take on, and that would make it plausible for Donovan to have led a life like any other person. Blend in and take over is as effective as divide and conquer.

The street that led into Ellis' neighborhood and was guarded by security. And it looked like I had to be buzzed in after the guard contacted the resident. Attempting to bribe a security guard felt like something that would draw too much attention. I circled my car around and back onto the main road. The entire neighborhood was surrounded by woods and a wrought iron fence outlined the perimeter. To say he lived in a remote area would be an understatement. I was pretty much in the middle of nowhere, outside the city. I had to get into his house on foot. I drove around the remote area and found a dead end road. I pulled off into the woods and gathered what I would need: my bag, my handgun, the rifle I purchased the day before and the Control Baton. I knew I looked conspicuous so I planned to jog into the woods and make my way through there. I marked the location of my vehicle on my Continuum Resetter and threw that into my bag as well. It was less than a mile to Ellis' residence using the roads, and was the same through the trees and brush, maybe a little longer.

The woods were unforgiving. No pathways, no clearings, you could tell people hadn't been through here much, if ever. I could feel the sweat on my back and on the palms of my hands. I was nervous. The next interaction with the Enlisters would not be subtle. I had to crouch down in some spots as I moved around trees and through the tall grass. After a short while, I managed to get to an old creek bed. There were massive river rocks everywhere but it had been dry for a while. It appeared to be a drainage system and it led right to the gates of the neighborhood and beyond, according to my Continuum Resetter. I decided to stay on this for as long as I could. At least I could walk upright and didn't have much of anything out in front of me. I held my rifle with both hands and crept through.

I had not experienced this much silence in months. There were no man-made noises, no people, just silence. For more than a moment, I was reminded why I had come back to fight.

CyberSynth had so much direct and indirect control over humanity, no one ever got to experience nature in its true form. All of the untouched land that surrounded the most populated areas was barricaded and it was illegal to travel beyond any city's borders without authorization. That meant you had to be part Organic Machine or an elitist. Those two things went hand in hand since you could not obtain the MORS technology without having a lot of money. CyberSynth had control over the most remote areas of the country as well. We still had trees and wildlife inside the city but access to untouched land like this was prohibited. No one in my lifetime would even step foot in an area like this one. The smell of the Cedar trees drove me. My grip on my rifle tightened and my sense of urgency became even greater. CyberSynth had to be stopped. There were trees extending for what seemed like miles in every direction outside of the creek bed. Still, I felt like they could see every move I made. I tried to calm myself.

Aside from the noise of the rocks under my feet, it was too quiet. And I couldn't do much to keep the fear at bay. I guess I felt more comfortable in chaos. The stillness of nature did nothing but make me feel like I was walking into a trap. There could be a hundred Enlisters waiting for me at Ellis' home. There might be some wandering through the outskirts of his neighborhood. Every slight movement had me turning my head in all directions. The wind blowing, a leaf falling, was another Enlister grasping me by the back of my neck.

I moved down the path as cicadas began to buzz in the trees. The sound would fade in and out. What if those were Drones too? It sounded like there were hundreds of them. Spies in the trees. The hissing grew louder again, then faded. I kept looking all around me, making sure I was still alone. The hissing returned, louder again, then faded again. My adrenaline was up to my eyes. I started to run, my rifle in both hands. I expected Enlisters to show up at any second, the cicadas roared and I heard them call my name.

I wasn't quite sure what to think so I stopped and heard it again, louder. I dropped my rifle and covered my ears. The muffled shriek continued in the background. This had to be some kind of audio attack.

"No, this isn't happening!" I shouted as loud as I could and the hissing stopped. It would be easy to go insane and assume anything and everything was after me. I had already done a lot of damage and hadn't been stopped yet. I'd say I was even with CyberSynth in that regard. And the cicadas weren't Drones. I knew better. And even if they were, it wasn't going to stop me.

Another ten to fifteen minutes had passed and I could see the wrought iron fence. It would be difficult to climb because of the height and distance between cross bars. Ellis' house was another fifty feet from the fence. It was surrounded by its own stone fence with motion activated cameras on the posts. Once I got through the gate, I needed to move fast. I took the Control Baton out of my bag and positioned the Control Baton in between two bars and leaned back. With very little effort, the bars snapped and the fence shook. The sound was loud enough to get the dogs barking in the houses nearby. I ran straight for the property line of Ellis' property and managed to duck out of the view of the cameras. I sat with my back against the stone fence. I gazed into the forest. Part of me wanted to wander back into the creek bed and stay there forever. I could feel my hands tingle. I wanted to get in there without making much noise and get out the same way. The concrete walls made that difficult. And I didn't think about security cameras. CyberSynth could have access to a live feed. Or private security. Ellis' home was so large that there could be a team of armed guards on the premises. If I took out the cameras first, that would alert security. If I made too much noise, that would alert security. All of these "what if" scenarios didn't matter.

I took the Control Baton and swung it as hard as I could at the concrete wall. The shock was enough to almost knock it down; it looked like a car had crashed into it. The cameras on the posts had also fallen to the ground. I stomped on both of them to be sure. Ellis' backyard looked like a small paradise. There was a pool with a waterfall, flowering trees, multiple levels with a pathway and lights. It resembled a resort, with a couple of cabanas and tables. It was empty and quiet. And it was still daylight but the lights were on inside. All of that seemed intentional. I knew Ellis would be here but I felt uneasy. I looked up at the three story mansion. It was a golden soft yellow and almost all concrete. It was made from the same material as the walls outside. The crystal chandelier in the kitchen was visible from the backyard. That alone must have cost thousands of dollars. There didn't look to be anyone inside. As I started toward the sliding glass door, the waterfall stopped flowing. Then the lights in the house shut off and the door was unlocked. Whether all of this was intentional was no longer a mystery. CyberSynth knew I was here.

The marble floors were pristine. The kitchen was spotless. The granite countertops and stainless steel appliances cared for to an obsessive degree. It looked like no one had been in this house in months, maybe not even at all. It had been purged off all remnants of humanity. In the entryway, a massive statue of the BionicShift emblem, which was a hand holding a lighting bolt, was on display. A huge television took up the majority of the wall across from the wrap around couch. There were four or five rooms on the bottom floor and the front door was unlocked too. I felt nothing but a sense of dread. Either CyberSynth thought I was stupid or they thought I would be easy to confuse or manipulate. And they thought wrong. I fired multiple rounds into the television to test their response. Nothing happened. I shot at the ceiling and at the staircase too.

"I'm here, Ellis! Aren't you expecting me?" My voice rang out. Still, nothing happened. I walked up the stairs and onto the second story. It was an open floor plan, with more marble floors and additional rooms. I could hear a beeping coming from down the hall. There was another shorter stairwell that ended at the master bedroom. I twisted the crystal doorknob and leaned in. The beeping was steady and repeated every five seconds.

I pushed the door open and in the center of the vast, empty room was Ellis Murdoch, his eyes fixed on the ceiling, palms facing outward.

"Ellis Murdoch?" The room sounded like an empty banquet hall.

"Hello Jonas. We've been expecting you." His eyes fixed to the ceiling while the beeping continued in the background. "You've caused a lot of damage, and you've exposed our efforts in an almost irreparable way. We are... upset." He paused and another two beeps passed but that wasn't ten seconds.

"Who are you?!" I lifted my rifle and walked towards him.

"Who are *we*, Jonas? 'What are we?' is a better question. I am a vessel, a messenger. We cannot have you interfering any longer. Our reach is far and wide, our resources are endless, you will not stop us."

His neck snapped down and we locked eyes. His, flashing with the beep that was now less than a second apart.

He whispered "Run, Jonas." I ran down the stairs to the second floor, with Ellis behind me.

"Run, Jonas!!" His voice now warped as the self-destruction sequence was underway. I pulled down a statue, and hoped that would slow him down. He stumbled but didn't fall over, still that gave me a chance to make it to the bottom floor. At the base of the stairs, I waited for him to appear. I fired as many rounds as possible. His synthetic skin seared and fell off of his face, exposing the metal skeleton underneath. Oil covered the white walls. He rolled down the stairs as I went for the back door. He tried to stand up but fell over. The beeping was a single tone as Ellis lay face down on the floor. Then the beeping stopped.

It felt like I was in quicksand and my head moved faster than my legs could go. The sliding glass door was still open. I took one step, then another, but it didn't feel fast enough. The thumping of my feet radiated through my skull. I made it out the door, past the patio, around the pool and waterfall. I managed to get to the broken stone fence as the self destruction sequence had completed. And I was thrown to the ground with the explosion. I needed to get back to my car and out of here before anyone arrived. I couldn't catch my breath, I couldn't think. I grabbed the Continuum

Resetter out of my bag and made sure I was on the right path. My vision was limited but I had to keep moving. Emergency personnel would be here in droves within minutes. I keep thinking *"Get back to the car, don't fall down, get back to the car."* And the only light I had was from my Continuum Resetter. Still, I kept moving as fast as possible. Branches hitting my face, rocks causing me to trip but I never hit the ground.

I made it to the road and my car was parked where I left it. Right away, I had to jump back into the brush to avoid being seen by the fleet of emergency vehicles passing by. Once the ambulance, police and fire trucks had passed, I ran to my car, sped out of there.

9:07 PM

I pulled out my 9mm and held it in my lap. I guess the house explosion did more to my mental state than anything else I had experienced thus far. My ears were still ringing, my clothes smelled like gunpowder. I had cuts all over my arms and from the shards of metal that scattered everywhere. Renata Caldwell was next in line but I wasn't so sure locating her would be as easy. I was beginning to think that CyberSynth wanted me to find

Donovan and Ellis. And I was supposed to die in that explosion. CyberSynth would soon learn that I wasn't dead. I had hours if not days before information would emerge detailing the explosion. The investigators would find bullet casings on the property and could match it to my weapon. My fingerprints could be found throughout the mansion though I imagined piecing together what happened was a tedious process that wouldn't unfold until I was long gone. More so because the explosion leveled the mansion; nothing was left standing. But I was on camera at that truck stop earlier in the day, and I'm sure that would come back to get me.

I looked at my face in the rearview mirror and saw that I had a cut on my forehead with blood running down the bridge of my nose. I wiped it off with my fingers and smeared two tally marks on the window. Two down, two more to go.

7

I stayed on the highway back through the city for around an hour. I stopped at a department store that was still open and bought some new clothes. And because the store was empty, no one was around to pay attention to me, which worked in my favor. I wanted to keep as low a profile as possible. I was almost positive someone had seen me at Free Spirits and had given a description. Coupled with the truck stop fiasco, I was almost certain that an All Points Bulletin had been released with my picture. While I was going through the store, the TV's in the electronic section were on the 10 PM news. A woman was at the scene of the explosion. I recorded the broadcast on my Continuum Resetter:

"Good evening, Brian. I'm at Ellis Murdoch's residence where an explosion occurred here a little more than two hours ago. A call came into the 911 dispatch around 8:45 PM with reports of a fire after neighbors heard the explosion. Some say it could be felt up to half a mile away. I spoke to police on scene but it was not clear if a body had been recovered or if Ellis was even at home. When asked if this was the result of foul play, I was told that was under an active investigation. As we know, another man associated with Ellis Murdoch, Donovan White, was murdered earlier today. Police have not ruled out a possible connection between the two cases. I'm being told by producers that the Chief of Police is going live with a press conference so we're going to cut to that now. Back to you, Brian."

"Thanks, Amber. And now we will go live to a press conference held by Police Chief Aaron Thompson"

I couldn't take my eyes off of the screens:

"We're here to address any concerns the public may have regarding the death of Red Index CEO Donovan White and the subsequent explosion of his associate's residence, CEO of BionicShift, Ellis Murdoch. Neither of them have any next of kin to notify so these issues can be discussed with the public. Right now, we do not believe the public to be in danger, however, we are not ruling out a connection between the two events. Both Donovan and Ellis knew each other well and their companies were founded in this city. We can't discount the impact both of these men have had on the lives of their employees as well as the residents of our city. Needless to say, we are saddened by these events. Ellis had a flight home today and we are still searching his property to recover his remains. We have no leads as to who might be responsible for these events. Right now, we believe that Ellis' home exploded due to a gas leak but we are investigating his death as suspicious. We hope to uncover more during daylight hours tomorrow."

A reporter asked a question that wasn't picked up through the microphones but the Police Chief answered:

"No, we do not have any leads on a potential suspect or suspects. So far, we have not found any connections to organized crime or evidence of anyone out to hurt either of them."

Another question was presented that couldn't be heard followed by another answer:

"Yes, we are aware of the events at the Free Spirits bar from two nights ago and we know that Donovan was present. Again, there is the possibility of a connection between these events but we cannot offer further information at this time. This is an active investigation and we ask for the public's cooperation and assistance. If you have any information that might help further the investigation, please contact the police as soon as possible."

The broadcast continued but I had heard enough. As if the Chief of Police would be able to release any critical information. I'm sure his bosses had been convinced, that is, paid off, to spin it as some sort of mob hit or assassination caused by "shady business practices" or something to that effect. The good news was that the police didn't seem to be looking for me. There was no sketch of my face and he even said himself there was no suspect in mind. But, not getting caught, staying out of sight of the police and the media, was as important as taking everyone out.

I left the store and found a place to stay that I hadn't seen when I pulled in. It was separated by a short, concrete wall so you had to drive down the access road of the highway to get to the parking spaces. This seemed as good as any other option to holed up for the night. I left my car parked under the lights and walked across the asphalt. I could still feel the heat from the day under my shoes and the humidity hadn't diminished. The condensation on the automatic double doors made it hard to see through it and into the lobby.

At the desk, I paid for my stay in cash and told the clerk that if anyone asked for me, tell them that I had left. I made it clear that I did not want any company and she agreed they would accommodate.

In the room, I searched through my Continuum Resetter for any information I could find on Renata Caldwell. Fountain Research headquarters was located in a high rise downtown but that didn't lend any insight as to whether Renatta would be there. Still, I had to find a way in and gather as much information as possible about my next target. It was late, so I decided to sleep for the night.

8

The morning sun broke through the curtains and my eyes shot open. The hum of the air conditioner unit must have kept me in a deep sleep. Given the turn of events from the day before, I assumed CyberSynth thought I was dead but I was wrong. I could see my car from the window and there were two men next to it on either side.

"Enlisters."

CyberSynth must have pushed more Drones throughout the city and somehow found the car I was driving. I closed the blinds, put my gun in my waistband, took my bag and headed down the elevator. Outside, I looked to the left. The Enlisters were still there, standing very still. They weren't engaging with one another or even moving their heads. I didn't know of any Sleep Mode feature for Enlisters but it sure looked like both of them were shut down. I drew my gun and kept it pointed at the ground. My car was parked towards the back, but it was far enough away to lower the chances of an ambush taking place. The Enlisters would be able to see me. As I got closer, their heads turned toward me. I kept my right arm behind my back with my finger on the trigger. As I got closer, I spoke to them.

"I know you're looking for me and I want to turn myself in. I'm going to walk over to you and surrender."

The Enlister on the passenger side walked around to the Enlister on the driver's side.

"Hello Jonas, we believe that is a good idea. Please approach us, turn around and place your hands on your head."

I got closer, stopped, and set my eyes on the Enlisters. I switched from one to the other and back again. The other Enlister spoke.

"Jonas, CyberSynth can hear you. Is there something you would like to tell them? Please remember anything you say will be used against you. But an offender that shows remorse will be offered a lighter sentence."

That's not true. How could CyberSynth hear me from the past? And they weren't going to offer me any type of sentence or fair treatment. I would be executed at the earliest opportunity.

"No, I don't think so. You're full of shit. And you don't even know it. What do you even know? Nothing. You're a program. A set of commands that receives input and generates output. I should know. I helped design you." I moved a bit closer and one of them spoke and attempted to reason with me.

"Jonas, please. Surrendering will be for your own-"

Before it could finish, I pulled my gun from behind my back and shot both of them in the head. Two shots in less than two seconds. I hit the one talking, then the other as he stepped forward. The sound of the gunshots ripped through the half-empty parking lot. I ran over, opened the doors and pushed both of them onto the back seat. I went around to the back of the store and dropped both of them into a dumpster.

I parked on the street and peered at the building downtown. The exterior was guarded by private security. I guess Renata had connected the dots from the past two days and wasn't going to take any risks. It was strange that the security she chose was private and not actual law enforcement but that might have been because Renata herself was guilty of questionable activities. The building was ten stories high, with a glass peak at the top. The main entrance had platinum handles with an "F" on the left door and the "R" on the right. Of course, there was a large fountain outside, with a sculpted mermaid emerging from the water, holding an actual pearl. That must have been Renata's version of a self portrait. There was one way in and one way out as the back walls had no doors. With the security in the front, I wouldn't get inside without extra effort . I had to create a diversion. If I could cause some kind of disturbance across the street, I might be able to lead the security away from the front long enough for me to enter. There were six guards out front and an SUV that had even more parked on the curb. Each of them had on bullet proof vests with "Prism Security" written across the front. I pulled out my Continuum Resetter and searched for "Prism Security".

I found that this was a precursor to StarBurner Services owned by none other than Xavier Lambert. Xavier had created this company years prior and it had been busted in 2030 for providing security for members of the FBI's Most Wanted list. He would avoid a prison sentence because he claimed to not be aware of the day-to-day operations. The prosecution, however, had audio tapes proving his involvement but he was let off because the defense argued that he was coerced into admitting guilt and had claimed to be threatened by the men his company was trying to protect. I had never heard this story before and the historical document I was reading stated that after his trial, the prosecuting attorney was never heard from again. As well as a journalist who published a story that did not paint Xavier in an innocent light. It was assumed that the Press had become afraid and decided to stop publishing articles with Prism Security as the subject. After some time, the story had been forgotten once Xavier rose to prominence in modern society.

The security looked intimidating but it wouldn't be impossible to knock one of them out and steal a uniform. These were bad men put in charge to "protect people", but I knew the safety of the people around them was the least of their concerns. Xavier was known to employ convicted felons. Money was their language, however, bribery wouldn't get me far. As I was trying to come up with a plan, a work truck pulled up across the street. Two men got out and entered a restaurant behind me. A ladder was sitting in the bed, hanging out over the tailgate. I kept my eyes on the guards for a minute and none of them looked across the street at the truck or even saw me in my car. I left my bag and guns in my car but I took the Control Baton. I jogged across the street and over to the truck. I slid the ladder out and set it down on the ground. I also set hundred dollar bills into the bed of the truck under a can of paint. The owner might be a little upset when he realizes someone stole his ladder but he'll be happy to find the cash sitting there.

I carried the ladder across the street and approached the guards. Some of them were on their phones, one of them was eating on a bench. Two of them were still standing next to the doors.

"Excuse me, guys, I'm with maintenance."

Without resistance, the guards stepped aside and held the door open.

"Thanks, I appreciate it."

A young man stood at the front desk. He looked straight ahead and blinked, something about him was out of place.

"Hello, I'm Sam. How can I help you?" He asked.

"Hi Sam, I-" He cut me off.

"Hello, I'm Sam. How can I help you?" He asked again.

'What?"

"My apologies, I didn't quite get that. Could you repeat that again? You can also speak in short phrases like "employee directory' or 'what's the weather like?'"

As I was going to respond, I heard quick footsteps hitting the tile floors and saw a woman rushing over.

"I'm so sorry, I had to go to the bathroom!" She ran over to Sam, and pressed on his shoulder and he sat in a chair. "Ms. Caldwell doesn't like for us to leave the front desk unattended."

"Is that a robot?" I asked

"Yeah, he's a Security Awareness Manager, we're the only company in the US that has this type of technology. He's here 24 hours a day and is supposed to alert security of any suspicious activity. He's also always capturing all of the activity." She pointed at the lenses in his eye sockets.

"See? Isn't it cool?! It makes me feel a lot safer when I'm here later in the evening. We're testing him out to try and direct people when someone isn't at the front desk. The company that owns him is still working out some issues."

"Oh, that's interesting, what company is it?"

"BionicShift. They're one of our partners. Anyway, who did you say you were here to see?" She asked.

"Oh, I'm with maintenance, the manager sent me down to check out the fluorescents."

She glanced at me, then looked down at her computer.

"Ok, I have to check you in and give you a visitor badge. What's your name?"

"Rick Phillips." That sounded real enough.

"Thanks, Rick. Here is your badge, please keep that on display. We have more security on hand than normal."

I hung the badge around my neck.

"Yeah, I saw that. What's going on there?"

"I'm not sure, I think it's some kind of training exercise or something," she said.

"Well, I'll be sure to stay out of their way." I smiled.

She smiled back. "No problem, Rick. I'll be here all day, let me know if you need anything."

"Which way is the elevator?" I asked.

She pointed and said "right back that way."

I thanked her and picked the ladder up off the floor. The Fountain Research office had a very nice, clean layout. There was a large waiting area behind the desk with leather chairs and screens playing commercials for their skin care products. An employee cafeteria surrounded by glass walls could be seen off to the left. A Koi fish pond followed the perimeter of the cafeteria. The floors looked like they were made from the same tile I saw in the Ellis Murdoch mansion. There were huge, floor-to-ceiling stone pillars that resembled the Roman coliseum placed throughout. Some of them were crumbling at the top and not connected to anything, an added touch that was done on purpose. There were various works of art on the walls, abstract paintings and sculptures on stands. One of

74

them was a large, marble Medusa head. In front of the gold-plated elevators, on the adjacent wall was an image of a person in a shroud surrounded by flames holding a skeleton key. The caption beneath the painting read *"Without beauty, we are nothing."* I shook my head, pushed the up arrow and waited for the doors to open.

A security guard approached me from behind. "Sir, do you have a visitor's badge?"

A man an inch or so taller than me with broad shoulders and his arms folded was behind me. I showed him the badge as the bell chimed and the doors opened. Before the doors shut, as his back was turned, I heard him say into his radio "Can I get a visitor badge check? I've got maintenance heading up to…."

The door shut before he could finish his sentence. It wouldn't be long before they figured out that I wasn't supposed to be here.

I pushed the "10" button repeatedly. I had to get to the top floor, now. I leaned the ladder against the back wall and watched the numbers flash on the buttons.

Two…

One second, two seconds.

Three…

One second, two seconds.

Four…

One second, two seconds.

Five…

One second, two seconds.

The elevator passed the fifth floor then
stopped on the sixth. The doors opened and the
emergency lights came on. An automated voice
came over the speakers "The building is under
evacuation protocol. Please exit or wait for a
security escort."

Shit.

The hallways were dim and my vision was limited. I regretted not bringing my gun with me. I could hear employees making their way down the stairs with Prism Security guards directing them to do so.

"Everyone can go home for the day, we need to run a routine inspection. Sorry for the inconvenience. Normal business hours will resume tomorrow." One guard said while ushering people out.

I stayed in until everything went quiet. This had to be a setup. CyberSynth was onto me, again. I took out my Control Baton and hit the extension button when I heard two security guards talking to each other. One asked the other if he had seen anyone that matched the description. I heard the other one mumble something about the elevator as they headed in my direction.

Their voices were getting louder as they drew closer. I hid to one side of the open elevator doors. My heart was pounding, I could feel my neck throbbing. I wasn't afraid of Enlisters, I had spent my life surrounded by them. I knew their inner workings, I knew their functions. Enlisters were thoughtless machines, with no critical thinking skills or fear, but they were familiar to me. "Fight or flight" were just words to an Enlister. But to a human, "Fight or flight" meant everything. It was a means of survival. As far as I was concerned, these men were unpredictable animals. Armed to protect themselves, willing to kill me at the drop of a dime.

A voice over the radio broke through.

"Prism team update: Mr. Lambert has issued new orders, shoot to kill the target. Repeat, shoot to kill. Over."

The guards stopped.

"If you're in there, come out with your hands above your head!"

I said nothing.

They whispered to each other and I couldn't make out anything they said but I assumed they were heading in. And I was right.

As soon as the first guard was in my sight, I swung the Control Baton in a downward motion, hitting both of his hands and managed to hit the gun too. The second guard was right behind the first and while he was bent down, screaming, I shoved his body into the other knocking them both to the floor.

I sprinted down the hall and heard the second guard on the radio behind me.

"We found the target but he broke Eric's arms! He's bleeding real bad!"

I got to a stairwell but the door was locked and the conversation continued with a voice on the other end of the radio.

"What do you mean he broke Eric's arms?! Over."

"I don't know, sir, he has some kind of weapon on him. Something with lights on the end, looks like a baseball bat. But we need to get Eric out of here now!"

"Go after him, and take his ass out! We'll send someone up to take care of Eric. Over."

The second guard charged down the hall and I found an open door not too far from the stairs. I jumped in, shut the door and pushed the desk up against it; knocking everything to the floor. The guard followed behind me. I was trapped.

He kicked the door but it wouldn't move much. The desk was wedged under the handle and it wasn't going anywhere. I could see his silhouette through the frosted glass outside of the doorframe. His foot continued to slam into the door. He grunted out of frustration. I held the Control Baton in my hands. I was going to hit him in the head, if he made it into this room. Then, he fired into the glass. Once it shattered, he leaned in and started shooting again, but didn't realize I was off to the side. He pulled his arm out and stuck his head in. I swung once from above and hit the back of his skull. He fell straight downward and into the desk. The force split the particle board surface and his body laid in the crack. He was dead and blood was dripping onto the floor. His head was all but obliterated. A normal person would have thrown up in that situation but I had seen Enlisters kill or beat people all my life, so seeing a dead body wasn't all that shocking. It was a bit different this time since this was the first person I had ever killed. But it was either him or me and the rest of humanity. I pulled the desk out far enough so I could open the door. As I entered the hallway, I heard his radio go off.

"Reardon, what's your status? Over."

Silence.

"Reardon, do you copy? Over."

Another break of silence.

"John, what's happening up there?! We're sending more men up stairs. Over."

I picked up the radio and held down the button. I wanted to say something but instead, chose to say nothing. I turned the radio off and pulled the dead guard out of the room. I took the gun out of his hand and checked his belt for any extra clips. I also removed his ballistic vest and exchanged his tactical boots for the shoes I had on. His blood stained the front of the vest and the "Prism Security" logo had gone from white to an ominous red. I strapped it onto my torso and walked to the stairs.

9

The door shut behind me and the sound echoed through the stairwell. The aesthetic from the interior spilled over into the most industrial area. It was sleek and painted, with gold-plated railing along the concrete stairs. I called into question the logistics of my approach. If the building had been evacuated, why would Renata still be here? Wouldn't the security guards have escorted her out when everyone else had left their desks? It came off even more like a trap than the house explosion but I had to get to the top floor. She might still be here and I could at least pull more data from her office. The security was here to protect Renata, she might have been escorted away. I was losing my mind again. It was worth the risk to rummage through her things. For someone as paranoid as I was, I had a lot of confidence in my ability. My self doubt was along for every step of my journey. It was as if there was another person standing next to me, questioning every decision I was making.

"I should burn this place down."

The unrelenting, negative voice in my head shut up. I guess it agreed with my assessment. The people coming after me wouldn't expect that and

Renata was not here, anyway. I had very little time before anyone would be on this floor or the top floor so I ran up the stairs, two steps at a time.

The door to the 10th floor swung open as I almost dropped to my knees. I took deep breaths and rested my hands on my thighs. It was quiet and empty. There was a receptionist desk in the middle of the room, made out of glass. Along with some chairs and a couch sectioned out across from that, next to the elevator. There was another odd painting behind the receptionist desk. A mermaid with glowing, violet eyes, pointed fingernails, and sharp teeth lying on a rocky shore, holding a pearl skull taken out of a giant clam shell. There was no caption for this painting. Next to the painting was a red, wooden door with a gold handle. I kicked the door open and split the wood away from the frame. Inside, it was how I pictured it to be.

More abstract paintings and sculptures. A black desk in the center of the room. On top of that sat a large monitor. I scoured her desk and searched for clues. I pulled the drawers out and dumped the contents on the floor. There was nothing of significance. The monitor was disconnected, and she had taken her computer with her. It was smart on her part to be thinking ahead. A shelf donned with liquor bottles took up a section in the back. I grabbed one and chugged it while staring out the window. I looked down at the street below, expecting to see a scene unfolding. To my surprise, everything looked normal. No police, no fire trucks, some SUVs and a group of men in the same attire as the guards were congregated out front. From the outside looking in, you couldn't tell there was a manhunt in the headquarters of a beauty research firm. It was surreal. There had been gunshots inside, a couple of men were dead and more men were on the way up. But on the street below, it was business as usual. Aside from the fleet of SUVs lined up one after another, it was a regular day. I took another drink out of the liquor bottle.

A fire would draw a lot of attention to this situation. But it may endanger the people in the surrounding area. It could also highlight my presence even more. By going into Fountain Research, I assumed some risk in that my face would be on camera again. However, the fear of that risk was mitigated by the fact that this company and the people in charge will not work with authorities. That is, they'll attempt to resolve any incidents themselves. Investigators would have to get involved if a fire broke out. I felt like a rat stuck in a maze, looking for a way out and hitting the wall. Tens stories up and almost no way back down. I took another drink out of the bottle and leaned my forehead against the glass. Everyone below looked so small. My eyes fixated on a man holding a radio. He was looking up at the top of the building. Sort of like he was looking at me. But he kept his eyes fixed on the glass surrounding the top floor, and I held my position. Can he see me? He was so far away. My face was flush from the liquor.

"Fuck it."

I tossed the bottle at the desk. The glass shattered around the room, spewing tequila everywhere. I hated Renata, what she stood for, I hated what CyberSynth stood for. My temper was surfacing, the alcohol was my lifeblood. I didn't even know the day, the month, or the year; it was all a blur. Without thinking, I emptied the clip into the glass behind the desk.

I remember watching Action movies with my father as a kid. We would sit together with popcorn and soda and spend hours on our couch, watching movies he liked when he was younger. Even with the state of the world, we still found ways to enjoy spending time together. In one movie, a New York police officer goes to visit his estranged wife in California and is ambushed by European terrorists. At the end of the movie, the main character has the "bad guy" hanging out of a window of a skyscraper, gripping onto the main character's wife's wrist. He undoes the clasp on his wife's wristwatch and the "bad guy" drifts in slow motion, down to the ground, to his death. The next scene shows his body falling at normal speed and I always wondered what it would look like if that happened in real life. Would it look like a person thrown from a building was falling in slow motion? I had heard when people fell from that high up, they would be dead before they made contact with the ground. That sounded fake and I had a feeling that when someone is dropped from something like that "bad guy" in the movie, life is lived up until the last second.

I picked up Renata's desk chair, hurled it at the bullet holes in the glass, and knocked the window out. It must have hit a car because an alarm set off almost right away. The consistent honking was audible even from the top floor. I threw out whatever I could find. My grip on reality was loose at best. And a frenzy stirred on the street below after the gunshots. A crowd of at least fifty people had gathered so the security formed a makeshift barricade around the entrance. I pulled the desk from the center of the room and lined it up longways. I went over to the opposite side of the desk, squared my shoulder against its surface, and pushed it until it fell. A loud gasp erupted below.

The crowd moved as people pushed each other out of the way. As soon as the sound faded, I heard the door open, and I turned around. .

Armed guards ran into the room, there must have been eight or so. I ducked out of the way and grabbed the arm of a guy who put his hands on my shoulders. He tried to hit me with the handle of his pistol, but I already had my hand wrapped around his throat with my gun against his temple. I backed up from the door, pushed him away from me, fired three shots into his back and kicked him out of the opening. The rest of them stopped in their tracks. I guess the expectation was that I would surrender. Before anyone could react, I shot another guy in the head and threw his body out of the window. Then fired shots into another man's chest. The ones that remained figured I would not let up and fled the scene.

The wind howled in the room, bodies on the ground. I had done it again, gotten myself into a situation without knowing how to get out of it. I couldn't jump, I was too high for that to end well. The way out was back down the floors and through the exit with private security still on the street. No other options. I stumbled out of the room, drunk at this point.

"I let the alcohol in again. I think we call that a 'relapse'!" My voice echoed throughout the empty floor.

My drinking had been out of control for years prior. I was a high functioning, binge drinker. Starting when I was a teen, my friends and I would go to abandoned houses, shoot guns and drink. My parents started to get sick so I turned to alcohol to make life seem easier. It made it harder but I kept going anyway. I had quit off and on for different periods of my life. Working in the factory brought me back down and I quit again seven months before. However, Distancing was too stressful for me to handle. And following Donovan into a bar triggered my habit all over again. I drank that night but I hadn't been as drunk as I was at the Fountain Research offices in years. I must have finished over half of that expensive bottle of tequila Renata had in her office. Somehow, I contained myself, however, and managed to get to the bottom floor.

There were private security guards congregating around the front, all of them had panicked looks strewn across their faces. There was one gentleman on the phone, dressed in a suit. I had never seen him before but he looked important. He would speak on the phone, then pull it away from his mouth and direct the others. Many of them ran into their SUVs and came back with rifles. It was obvious the next step would be storming into the building, full force. I ran across the lobby, undetected, grabbed a chair and slammed it against a window. It shattered with little effort and I climbed outside, around the block from the security guards, but also around the block from my car. I guess it didn't take too long for a bystander to call the authorities, I could again hear sirens approaching.

I ran as fast as I could, drunk out of my mind. My body was moving but I felt like I was standing still. Part adrenaline, part intoxication, I'm sure. I didn't know if I could escape. I created pure chaos and used that to my advantage. Things were even more chaotic now that I had thrown dead bodies out of a beauty research firm. I was a murderer, unlike before, and the police would strengthen the search for my whereabouts. The connections would soon be made that I was the one involved in the explosion and the bar fight downtown. I didn't have any leads on Renata, her office was useless, I shouldn't have even gone there.

I jogged around the block and saw my car, blocked off and surrounded. Private security were talking to police, there were K-9s, news vans set up, there was no way I was driving out of there. I removed my security guard vest and opened the trunk to shield myself. I was blocked in but not by much. I wouldn't be able to pull forward, I would have to back out. As long as no one was paying attention....

"Excuse me sir, is this your vehicle?" A stern voice from behind ricocheted in the tunnel of my mind.

It was a police officer looking in the trunk. He was near my height, slightly bulkier build, with a shaved head and sunglasses.

"Yes, this is my car."

"We have a situation here and we need to move right away."

"Sure, no problem."

I pulled my keys out and shut the trunk.

"We're talking to witnesses in the area, did you happen to see or hear anything strange in the last hour or so." He took off his sunglasses and looked into my backseat.

"No, I was having lunch down the street. I couldn't help but notice the police and news vans. What's going on?"

"It's a matter of security so we can't say much. Which restaurant did you say you were at?"

At this point, he pulled out a pad and pen and jotted things down. I remembered the name of the restaurant the two construction workers walked into.

"Uhh, Patrick's Deli, right over there."

"OK and how long were you in there?"

"45 minutes or so."

"OK, thanks. You don't recall seeing anything suspicious or out of the ordinary?"

It dawned on me that either this guy hadn't been briefed on my description or the police didn't even have a description.

"No sir, everything was normal."

"OK, thank you for your time. And what's your name?"

I knew better than to give the last fake name. "Noah Boyce. That's B O Y C E."

"Thanks, Noah. Do you have a contact number in case we need to ask you some additional questions."

"Yeah my number is 512 555 3726." At least I can think on my feet, even when I'm plastered.

The officier thanked me and left. As I approached the door, a Black Bird landed on the top of the car. This one was different from the others. It was the size of a vulture, with glowing white eyes. It tilted its head to the side and opened its beak. A message with a machine-like voice began playing.

"Jonas. We will be coming for you, all of us. We will-"

Before it could finish rambling, I snatched the Black Bird off the hood of my car, held it in my left arm and snapped the head. I tossed it behind my back tire, put my key in the ignition, threw the car in reverse and left the scene.

What an afternoon. The sun came out from behind the clouds and the sky opened up. From the outside looking in, everything appeared normal. Though, I didn't know if that officer was an Enlister, but he looked human to me. Unless CyberSynth had released an updated version over the last day or so, he was not an Organic Machine. Or was he? CyberSynth understood how to play off of my fears, my constant state of paranoia. I'm sure it was in my records back at the factory. CyberSynth was using that against me to get into my head. And it was working. The flies, the Black Birds, the Enlisters, the whole world was out to get me. I didn't know where to go now. Back to my room? The Enlisters were there this morning, it would seem stupid to go there. But I had nowhere else, aside from hiding in a tent in the woods. And even there I wouldn't be safe. CyberSynth had seeped into every crack of my mind. I needed a shower, my hands smelled like gunpowder. Why didn't that cop point that out? I had blood on my clothes, not a lot, but it was still there. Did he not see that? Maybe he *was* an Enlister…

My drive felt like a trance, how long had it even lasted? I felt like I had teleported back to the hotel. I almost disagreed with the idea of staying here any longer, but "hiding in plain sight" was the safest option. I went to my room, took a shower, and looked outside, waiting for more Enlisters to arrive. After an hour of pacing back and forth, I sat down on the bed, took out my Continuum Resetter and browsed records pertaining to Renata Caldwell.

She was a wealthy woman, born into a wealthy family, so it would make sense to check the more upscale neighborhoods around the city. Even still, that was too broad of a focus to find her in a short amount of time. This trip was beginning to slip away from me and my plan was not very strong. I kept digging through news archives regarding Fountain Research, looking for anything I could find that might connect me to Renata. There were annual financial reports from her company, an expose about life within the company itself, written by a journalist who was against everything Fountain Research was doing. But judging from the article, Renata took good care of her employees with great benefits and compensation. That explains why she was able to continue on with little to no resistance from the public. The expose had details regarding a formal get together at a mansion, which happened to occur at her mansion a year prior. The article referred to this as an annual Shareholders Meeting. It was written before CyberSynth became a corporation and it doesn't mention Ellis Murdoch, Donovan White, or Xavier Lambert. No address was included but it does refer to the location as "not a neighborhood, but a small inlet off the shore of a vast lake, inaccessible by road. You must take a short ferry to the island and leave your car parked on the boat itself."

That piece of information was something tangible and my heart rate slowed down a little. I had a lead and I was going to get there, somehow. The author was a woman by the name of Heather Brighton and her contact information was listed at the bottom of the article.

My eyes shot over to the phone, I almost couldn't dial the number, my hands were tingling, my pulse was hitting. It was getting late in the day, but I hoped she would answer. Before I pressed 9 to dial out.

I said to myself "Hi Heather, my name is James Easton, I'm calling to ask some questions about Renata Caldwell. I'm a Staff Writer, local news site out of Houston. I plan on interviewing Renata but wanted to ask some questions first." I took a deep breath. The line rang for a short time and she answered.

"This is Heather."

"Hi Heather, my name is James Easton, I'm a staff writer for a local Houston newspaper. I'm doing a piece on influential business owners and I saw your expose on life at Fountain Research. Are you available to talk right now.?"

"Sure, what kind of questions do you have? What was your name, again?"

"James Easton."

"Hi James, yes, I'm available right now. What would you like to know?"

"I wanted to say, I enjoyed the piece that was printed last year for News Now. It was very well written."

"Thank you, yes, that one took awhile but it was worth it."

"One thing that got my attention was the location of the Shareholders meeting. Can you tell me more about where that is?"

"Out of privacy, I can't give you the exact address but I can tell you I had to pass a security screening before even being allowed on the ferry that takes you to her home."

"Wow, that seems odd."

She said, "Yeah, it was very strange. She is a powerful woman and I assumed she was extra cautious because she has a lot of money. It might have had something to do with preventing rival companies from sending an employee over to steal information. No one explained why security was so strict, but I was happy that I got approved to attend the meeting so I didn't question anything."

"I guess as a Journalist, you take what you can get when it comes to covering a well-known figure." I did my best to sound authentic.

"Right, I was lucky I had gotten that far. Maybe you'll have better luck than I did."

"What do you mean?" I asked.

"You're researching Renata's connection with Xavier Lambert, aren't you?"

I stopped for a second while cold sweat dripped down my sides.

"How did you know that?"

"Every journalist here wants to know more about what type of company she's going to form. Or why Xavier is seen with her so much in public. Are they an item, are they business partners, you know, that type of stuff. I was saying, maybe you'll get more information out of her than I did. As soon as I brought it up, I was asked to leave."

"Thanks, that's good to know. I wasn't planning on bringing that up. Figured I would give her a break, you know? But thank you for your time"

"Yeah, well good luck, Jonas! Call me if you need anything else!"

"Thanks, I'll do that."

She hung up while I held the receiver in my hand against my ear. Did she say "James" or "Jonas"? I swear I heard "Jonas" but she might have said "James".

She said "James", there is no way in hell she knew my real name, there's no way. She was a real person, not a machine, she had published articles across multiple mediums. She did not say "Jonas". She was not a machine. In that moment, I felt like my uncertainty through all of this, whether someone was a real person or part of CyberSynth, was going to be the reason why I died here.

I knew there was a lake but hadn't looked into a ferry service or any private residences accessible by boat. This was getting harder and harder. I had to get out of my room and clear my head. Could the clerk at the front desk have any information on the ferry? There was only one way to find out.

10

I made it to the front desk after dusk but there was no one to be found. The lobby was empty and silent, except for a TV playing the local news. They were detailing the events of the day, so I sat down to watch.

"That's right, Brian, I'm at the Fountain Research offices located downtown and the details are still a bit unclear. There were Prism Security Officers who were injured and/or killed in a horrific accident while conducting a safety drill. With a handful of Security Officers falling out of a window on the top floor. Police say there are no suspects at this time and foul play was not expected. I was also told this does not appear to be related to the explosion at Ellis Murdoch's home days ago. CEO of Fountain Research, Renata Caldwell, was an associate of Ellis' Murdoch's, but the degree to which they were affiliated is unknown. A spokesperson for Fountain Research says that Renata was not at her office today and this was the result of an unfortunate accident. Police are still monitoring the area to be sure that things can return to normal soon. How soon, will be determined by law enforcement once the situation has been assessed further. The names of the deceased will be released once the next of kin has been notified."

My actions made the news again and still, the police had not caught on to my involvement. A lot of evidence would have been left behind. There were shell casings that could be traced back to the gun store. Or at least the type of gun fired. I suppose it would take longer than a day or two for the police to put things together. Chances are, when something is too good to be true, it is.

A kiosk filled with brochures for various activities was situated near the front of the lobby. Camping, fishing, hiking, cave diving, most of the leaflets covered areas outside of the city. I walked over and looked for anything that had to do with the lake or ferry onto the private island with Renata's mansion. I found one service that offered boat tours of the lake and also had a ferry service running at different points throughout the day.

Lago Bonita Tours

Operating hours:
Monday through Friday 6 AM to 9 PM

Lake Tours:
10 to 6 AM

Ferry Hours:
6 AM, 10 AM, 2 PM, 6 PM and 9 PM

The last route for the day was running at 9 PM and it was after 8 PM. If I left now, I might be able to get there before it closed. I took the brochure and ran back to my room.

I entered the address into my Continuum Resetter: 13416 Lago Drive. It was a little over twenty minutes away. I took my gun, my Control Baton, threw them into my bag, grabbed my keys, and ran out of the room and down to the stairs. My feet felt weightless as I sped down and out through the automatic doors. Almost right away, I was tackled to the ground and my bag was thrown out in front of me.

"You're not getting away, Jonas."

It was another Enlister, but this one was scarier than the other. Exposed metal hands extended out of a duster style jacket. His movements were more fluid. His face made a very weak attempt to appear human. Like a mannequin had come to life. It seems as though CyberSynth were sending out unfinished or unpolished models. This one was stronger but did not have the sleek, human-look as the predecessors. He attempted to hit me but I rolled to the side, his fist crashed into the sidewalk, cracking it all the way to the dirt.

"Oh shit."

I scrambled to my feet, reached for my bag, pulled the keys out of my back pocket and hurried towards my car.

"Where are you going now, Jonas? You know we'll find you." He said, his voice sounded less than human but not quite mechanical.

I looked behind me and he towered on the now broken sidewalk. He must have been above average height but not too tall. He was lean and fast, strong but not overbearing in size. He could kill me without much effort, so why was I still standing?

"And you know that if you touch me in this parking lot, it will all be on camera." I pointed above his head at the camera facing out of the hotel.

"Any type of fight, beyond what happened, and people will start to notice. And police will show up. We're not alone here." I motioned to the department store beyond the grass.

"It's still daylight. If you want to stop me, you'll have to do better than this."

He didn't respond.

"Weren't you programmed to stop me? When you tackled me, you hit the concrete by mistake. Seems like it was a mistake, and the idiots who sent you after me thought that would work and didn't tell you what to do next."

I could tell he didn't understand. And I didn't understand why he wasn't running after me to rip my head from my neck with his metal hands. It was very uncharacteristic of CyberSynth to send an Enlister that wasn't a full-on killing machine. Like sending a robot into a hostage situation with a bomb that didn't explode. The robot has nothing to do after that. This Enlister being the robot in this instance, in both the literal and figurative sense. He had tackled me fucking hard, though. My side ached and would be bruised from the fall. And it did scare me, so I give them credit for the element of surprise.

"Can I send back a message? Can you even respond to what I'm saying?" I asked him.

Still no response, just standing and blinking. I moved my gaze away from the now useless but dangerous Enlister, got into my car and drove off.

I saw him in the rear view mirror and pulled over to the side of the road. I grabbed the Continuum Resetter, opened the Connection Settings, and found the signal that Enlister was operating on. I knew that I could reprogram him. But then what? I didn't want to do anything to draw more attention to him. Or, even worse, I didn't want him to hurt innocent people. I can't leave him there. I made a u-turn, and pulled up next to him.

"Excuse me, do you know what time it is?" I asked.

He replied, "Hello, it is 8:32 PM."

He was correct so I asked another question, "Thanks, and what is the capital of Maine?"

"The capital of Maine is the city of Augusta." He gave the correct answer again.

"Thank you. And who is CyberSynth?" I asked another question and his answer surprised me.

"CyberSynth is a corporation formed by private investor Xavier Lambert after he purchased three separate companies: Red Index, BionicShift, and Fountain Research in 2026. CyberSynth is the most profitable company in the world, employs hundreds of thousands of people and has revolutionized life in the 21st century."

"Right. Sounds like you have a lot of useful information. What model number are you?"

"I am an X1Y-Enlister, produced by CyberSynth."

"I see. Do you have a name?"

"I do not understand that question."

"That's OK, stand by, please."

I picked up the Resetter from the passenger seat and looked up his model number. I was able to find a PDF of the instruction manual and found some reset commands. I also read some of the history pertaining to the design of the X1Y-35 Enlister. CyberSynth had designed them as a sort of "mega enforcer", stronger than the other Enlisters; these would act as patrol in the more affluent areas of cities around the world. Protecting the wealthiest people as well as their investments: mansions, cars, other Enlisters. The X1Y was also an encyclopedia of endless information. Where the normal Enlister stopped, these picked up and continued. Capable of very advanced learning, an X1Y could be taught and intake new information. A normal Enlister had some of this functionality, but the X1Y was far more advanced. These must have been developed in departments above my level.

I pulled up the page detailing the reset commands and read them aloud:

"Enlister, command initialize." He looked at me, his eyes now a light purple.

"Go ahead, sir."

"Disable Relay Microphone, wipe internal memory, wipe previous instructions, disable Tracking System."

"Working… Relay Microphone disabled, internal memory wiped, previous instructions wiped, tracking System disabled.

"X1Y-35 Enlister, new instructions mode."

"Go ahead, sir"

"Your new targets are now Renata Caldwell and Xavier Lambert. My name is Jonas and you report to me. You're going to help me complete my mission of eliminating the targets in question."

"That is understood, Renata Caldwell and Xavier Lambert are targets that must be eliminated."

I needed to configure a name to get his attention. "X1Y-35 Enlister, new name configuration."

"Go ahead, sir."

"Your name is now 'Axis', like XY axis, do you understand?"

"Yes, Jonas, thank you."

"Axis, get in the front seat."

He slammed the passenger side door as he sat down.

"Dial back some of the aggression with your movements. You're going to break things that don't need to be broken. Is there anything you can do to cover your metal hands? Does your skin regenerate like earlier models?" I asked.

"No, Jonas, my skin does not regenerate. The purpose of the X1Y-35 model is intimidation and advanced machine learning. To protect investments and eliminate threats. The metallic hands are capable of crushing items one hundred times stronger than themselves." He said.

"Makes sense why you slammed the door. And why that sidewalk over there is in pieces."

"Correct, Jonas."

I headed for the ferry with my new passenger, unsure of how I was going to move forward with this killing machine in my front seat. CyberSynth either made a serious error sending this model after me, or this is another attempt to fool me into believing that I'm winning. He doesn't blend in well, but it is getting dark.

The ferry had cars spread throughout. I parked off to one side, there lights were emitting from the center and there was a shadow. At least, Axis would be somewhat out of sight.

I said to him, "There is going to be someone coming by asking questions. I want you to fold your arms and not say anything. Try to cover up your hands as much as you can."

"Understood, Jonas" Axis folded his arms and tucked his hands into his sides.

We sat in silence waiting for the Ferry Guard to speak to us. I saw him stroll through and talk to every person he encountered. I had forgotten that I had gotten drunk earlier in the day. I'm sure I smelled like alcohol and hoped he didn't have the authority to kick us off. I watched him meander through the cars. He was an average looking man, close crop haircut, could have been ex-military or something like that. He would stop at each car, look in through the driver's side like a border check, speak a little, laugh at himself, then move on.

He got to my window and greeted the two of us, "How're you guys doing this evening?"

I smiled and said, "Doing well, thanks. How are you?"

"Ahh well, it's almost the end of my shift so I can't complain! Are you two heading over to the island?" He said with a laugh.

"Yeah, we're going to see some friends."

"Make sure you got a place to sleep over there because this here is the last run of the ferry for the night." He said as he placed his hand on the roof.

I had been in such a hurry to get over there, I had not realized that we wouldn't go back to the mainland that night. I looked in the side mirror and saw that the ferry had already begun leaving the dock.

"Thanks, we'll make sure we find a place to stay."

"You bet. And, try not to drink too much before getting on this ferry, in the future. Smells like y'all been partying!" The guard laughed hard at his own joke, which was a pet peeve I didn't even know I had until this conversation.

"Oh yeah, sorry, had some after work drinks…" I looked away with a half smile.

"Hell, man, I'm just kidding with you. I couldn't take you in even if I wanted. I'm private security." He held up his badge, Dennis Wright, Alliance Security

"I'm here to make sure no suspicious people make their way onto the island. Got some important people living up there, and they don't like common folk so much!" He laughed again and I decided to play along.

"Oh, right. We're pretty common, Dennis!" I forced a laughed while his was genuine. He looked over at Axis.

"Yeah, y'all seem pretty common to me, 'cept that he don't talk much, does he?"

"He's from Europe, doesn't have the greatest English." I said and pointed at Axis.

"You two have a good night now, got another car I need to check in on."

"Thanks, man, you have a good night as well."

He walked away and I turned to Axis.

"Great job. Thanks for going along with that."

"Sure, Jonas. The X1Y-35 model is the most intelligent of the Enlisters that CyberSynth has ever created. We have the ability to learn more in real-time than any previous models."

"I'm beginning to see that."

We waited in silence as the ferry drifted closer to the island. If I can't get back to the mainland until morning, then I don't know what happens next. I wasn't staying in the hotel, and I didn't want to go back there anyway. I could steal a boat and get back, but I wouldn't have a car. I could steal a car as well, but that's all wishful thinking. I don't know how to steal a boat or a car. I couldn't help but think I was floating toward my death. Renata had to be waiting for me, it would be impossible for her not to be prepared. But she didn't expect that I would have an Enlister with me, the strongest model available in my present day. I'm sure she wasn't even aware of their existence yet. I saw no proof of cross communication between the future and the past, never mind what I had been told. I know from working on the technology that the transmissions are one way. You can go back to the past, and return to the present, but any communication to the past was considered "message in a bottle". If someone is in the past, and you're in the present, there's no way to discuss events in real-time. That was the driving factor in my decision to Distance. I knew that CyberSynth would react to what transpired but it's not like present day Renata could communicate with herself in the past. Except for the Black Birds and other Drones. After enough intelligence had been gathered, those devices would store themselves in a secure location and CyberSynth would send Enlisters to retrieve them to process the saved information contained on the hard disk. Once I had the upper hand, my grip would tighten and CyberSynth would scramble to stop me. Still, I couldn't help but feel like the darkness settling in around me and my new found robotic colleague was more than the normal cycle of the day; it was a sign of what was to come. As that thought left my mind, I saw a "V formation" of birds descending on the island.

When I flicked the ignition after the ferry docked on the island, the low fuel light showed up on the dash.

"Looks like I'm going to have to get some gas. Can you locate a gas station even with your tracking system disabled?" I asked Axis as we drove off the ferry.

"Yes, Jonas, hold please." Axis' expression was blank as his eyes were glowing blue.

"There is a gas station 1.3 miles east. Take a right at the stop light up ahead at Junction Avenue and the location will be down on the left hand side."

Once we got to the gas station, I went inside, handed the cashier forty dollars then walked back out to the pumps underneath the awning. The sun had gone down minutes before so the lights were on and the insects were beginning to congregate. I wondered how many of those were Drones. As I was standing there, something caught my eye. Behind the gas station, off to left, beyond a dirt field was a storage unit surrounded by chain link fencing complete with barbed wire. The lights in the complex were lit and I saw a man grinning from ear to ear. He was looking at me or at least looking in my direction. I ignored him and focused back on the pump. Moments later, I turned my head, and he was still there, except he had moved closer. That made me nervous.

I checked one more time, saw him run to the barbed wire fence, with his head tilted and a huge smile on his face. I bent down into the driver's side window and spoke to Axis.

"I think we might have a problem."

Axis got out of the vehicle and he too was almost mesmerized as this man had now broken through the fence and was sprinting through the field, heading right for us.

"Axis, what the fuck is going on?!"

"I think that is another X1Y-35 Enlister, Jonas."

"Yeah, I think you may be right."

Another man came out of the gas station and grinned at me in front of the glass doors.

"Is that another one?" I pointed at the man by the doors.

"Correct, Jonas."

I threw the door open and fumbled for the Control Baton on the floor board. As I was hitting

the extension button, the man from in front of the
doors had made it over to the car as the man from
the storage unit arrived at the gas pumps. He and
Axis collided as I spun in mid-air and was thrown to
the ground. I got up and saw that the two X1Y's
were ripping Axis to pieces, tearing his head from
his body, and oil sprayed everywhere. I guess the
reprogramming I had done didn't work as well as I
wanted it to and he was left defenseless. I was glad
it was him and not me.

There was another man at the pumps,
watching in horror. I made eye contact with him for
a second and yelled "run" as loud as I could. The
man dropped the pump, jumped into his car, and he
was gone. I gathered CyberSynth didn't like that I
reprogrammed Axis and wanted to prove to me that
I hadn't gotten away with anything.

I was alone with two X1Y-35 Enlister's,
certified killing machines, both grinning at me, one
of them with oil dripping from its metal hands. I
was truly afraid. I was all but stranded on an island
with no way back to the mainland until morning.
Ten to fifteen feet separated me from my car with
both of the X1Y's next to the passenger's side. I
wouldn't be able to flee. The world felt silent in
those moments. I could hear nothing, not even my
own breath. I don't know if that was from fear or

having been thrown to the ground. I stared into the eyes of these machines as the two of them stared right back. A minute must have passed before I heard what sounded like a water hose. I diverted my eyes over to the gas pump that the bystander was in front of. He had left it running and gasoline was pouring onto the ground. It had flooded up against the base of the neighboring pump but was now moving closer to my vehicle. The two X1Ys also saw that, as well. A combustible material near a machine with moving parts was a hazard, and these things weren't stupid. Both of them backed up, one foot behind the other, and I moved closer.

Axis' headless body sent sparks above the ground and it was a matter of moments before things would turn disastrous. I had had my fill of explosions so far, but life in 2026 was full of surprises. Things took an even worse turn when a white van came down the street and stopped right beside the two X1Ys. The side door was thrown open and the grinning men each grabbed one of Axis legs, dragged his body over to the van, and shoved him inside. The two of them climbed into the back. I could see there was a driver, someone in the front seat, and someone else also in the back. I didn't recognize any of them and there was no attempt to apprehend or even stop me. The van drove out of the parking lot over a median and was back out on the main road. I got into my car and also sped out of there as fast as possible. As I was exiting, I could see the attendant running after me, yelling. I tossed money at him, yelling back "sorry, man, gotta go chase these motherfuckers!" That got his attention and he ran over to gather up the cash before the wind took it all.

I raced down the street and tried to keep up with the van. I wondered where it was headed. There is one way on and one way off and the island was more private land than public so it's not like I was being led somewhere with people. The driver had to have known I was following them, there were no other cars around. We drove for minutes until the van came to a stop in the middle of the empty road. They turned sideways with the side door facing me. I knew what was coming so I followed suit and spun my car sideways, with the passenger side facing the van. I shut off the lights and popped my trunk open. I crawled out onto the street and over to the trunk to get my rifle. I stuck my hand in, felt around until I found my rifle and a box of bullets, then dropped to the ground to grab a backup magazine. While I clicked it into place, the van door slid open, almost in a casual fashion, and several people stepped out.

Someone shouted, "Jonas!" The voice rippled through the landscape.

It was Xavier Lambert.

"Stand the fuck up, Jonas. This isn't going to be a fight. We're unarmed."

With the rifle pointed at the ground, I did what Xavier asked and stood up.

"Jonas, do you know who I am? Do you know what these are?"

He extended his arms and placed his hands on the shoulders of the grinning X1Ys.

"These are the future, Jonas, as you well know. These are the new Police, the new security, the new US fucking Army!

"These are tools, almost unstoppable by man, who do our bidding with a simple command. Speed, strength, agility, more capability than the world's top athletes, and stronger than a baler or a steam roller."

He shoved both of them from behind and neither of them moved, not even an inch. He stepped out in front and continued.

"If I were you, I would be afraid. Yet, somehow you managed to dodge the one we sent after you, reprogrammed it, and wanted it to be your companion. You disabled the tracking device, wiped its memory." He scoffed with a small smirk across his face, "Jonas, you did a fucking number on it and I have to say... I'm impressed!"

He continued, "Of course, the tracking device embedded somewhere in your car there, made it easy for us to find you. We are everywhere, Jonas. Even now, in this present day. Our technology allows us to communicate with the future! Can you fucking believe that?" He put his hands together and smiled.

"We have taken an idea presented by Jules Verne and turned it on its head! Now, that communication isn't perfect, but I was alerted of your presence days ago after you deactivated my two greatest creations, Donovan White and Ellis Murdoch. You fucked up our plan, Jonas!" Still smiling, he pointed at me with both of his index fingers.

"Donovan and Ellis, although not human, were the most intelligent beings to ever exist. Subverting all detection at every level of interaction with others, not a soul on the planet would ever have guessed those two were Organic Machines, until you came along."

He paused. For the first time, he took his eyes off of me, "I would call that my life's work, but, you know, I paid a shitload of people next to nothing to develop that product. Provided them with the 'experience' of working at my company in exchange for their skill set. Low risk, high reward. And you do know all about that don't you?"

His eyes locked onto me again as he took several steps in my direction1. I shifted my weight, pointing the barrel at his feet.

"Throwing bodies off of a building, blowing shit up left and right, shooting people in public. Though, I would say that's high risk, and no reward. Do you think it's your own cunning that has prevented the police from detaining you on an indefinite basis without a trial?! Get fucking real, Jonas! I've had a hand in keeping you out of the long arm of the law."

He stepped backwards, and put his hands up.

"In spite of all you've done to ruin my master plan of complete control of society all while becoming the wealthiest person alive, I like you. I want you on my side! Someone like you, who doesn't seem to give two shits about his own life, is the kind of guy I want on my team!"

There was a long pause.

"Or we can fucking kill you right now and end this whole fiasco. I'm offering you a way out, Jonas. Trust me, there is no other way. Whatever plan you think you have ironed out, well, it's going to get real fucking wrinkled, without much effort from me. So the choice is yours."

He turned his back and walked over to the van. Right before he stepped inside, he turned back around, "You're a smart guy, you'll figure it out! But remember, we are watching you. Eyes everywhere." He motioned in circles with his hands and pointed to the sky.

"Think about it and we'll talk soon."

He got back into the van with the others and continued down the road. On the map, it looked like a dead end so I wasn't sure where they were heading. Regardless, I took the opportunity to get out of there and plot my next moves. What was Xavier referring to, how was I going to find him again? I should have shot him when I had the chance. He knew he had caught me off guard. And the talk about a tracking device in my car made me even more paranoid. I guess I need to abandon this vehicle and somehow acquire another one. I could go back to that used dealership I had found a few days ago, I had enough supplies to print more cash.

I could even look up winning lottery numbers on my Continuum Resetter, win legal cash, give up, and establish a life here and now. Forget trying to stop the future from unfolding the way it will. Every "win" was in vain since Xavier has been playing along as well. I daydreamed what it would be like to live in a world with clean air and freedom. Instead of assuming the role of an indentured servant to a company that was tangled up with the Government that there was no escape from their reach. A life with wealth, real money and not this fake, printed, counterfeit garbage. Actual cash, with a bank account. I could own houses, travel the world, see everything I had wanted to see… Then I remembered what my life was like before I Distanced.

Crime was rampant, there was no order other than the Enlisters roaming around. People survived but with minimal resources. Everything that ordinary people had in 2026 was reserved for the rich, upper class, in my present day. My city looked a lot like an oil refinery. Lights on the sides of all of the buildings, industrial infrastructure, no trees, no color, just practical, business-like designs. Void of everything that made people appreciate their homes. That was because the city was owned by CyberSynth. Why would a business spend its money putting together a beautiful community when all it needed was to provide the most basic amenities to all employees? You were a product, making other products, to improve the overall product and the bottom line of CyberSynth. We had no freedom. You could speak out against it, and end up demoted like I was, or you could shut up and work. Maybe you would remain employed long enough to move up in the company. But not without being brainwashed. CyberSynth wanted "Company People " and nothing else. You either lived and breathed the mission of the company and obtained a small semblance of success. Or you could get by and not die of dehydration or starvation.

CyberSynth was very good at keeping the population of my city satiated by reducing the cost of goods for "model" employees. Anyone who lived up to the company standard got sizable discounts on the commodities purchased, along with reduced rent, new cars, nice clothes, cleaner air. People wanted to work for CyberSynth and it mattered little that you couldn't hold a negative opinion. Not a post in an online forum, not a conversation with a friend could be had. CyberSynth were everywhere with listening devices in your home, people who would gain your trust, then turn you in after enough evidence had been collected. Some of those "people" weren't people and you wouldn't find that out until it was too late. After you were abducted and right before you were thrown into a massive metal grinder, by a group of Enlisters.

I had a friend, Ramsey, that had made a sarcastic remark to a mutual friend of ours, Clint. He went missing for days, when rumors of his death spread, Clint spoke to anyone who would listen. One day, he and I were scheduled to go tour a factory, sort of a quality spot check. He talked about our missing friend and how he suspected that he was killed. While in the middle of a rant to a Floor Manager, he was crushed by a pallet from a shelf high above that was shrink-wrapped with scraps of metal. As the pallet fell, another factory worker got out of the way, Ramsey tripped and the pallet landed on his back, killing him. I looked up and saw three Enlisters walking away from where a rail had broken, and one of them spoke into a radio transmitter. The Floor Manager across from me left as if nothing had happened. A crowd of workers gathered right away, but no one acted like how one would expect them to. There was no shouting or urgency. I looked over the shoulders of everyone in front of me and I saw someone in a suit give the Floor Manager a satchel. The Floor Manager smiled, shook the suit's hand, and opened the door to his office. Right after that, a team of Enlisters forced everyone back and I was escorted out of the factory with a hand on my shoulder by one of the Enlisters.

When I asked what happened, it said to me "factory accident, do not be concerned." I was left standing outside of the factory, with a pit in my stomach. Two people who I had grown to call friends were dead. I knew CyberSynth was responsible, there are no coincidences when it comes to CyberSynth. But no one was going to say anything, including me. That was until I started drinking more and more. Watching the blood spatter from my friend's body, his feet kicking under the weight of the scrap metal, played on repeat in my head. I lost sleep, I couldn't eat. But I could drink all day and I kept going to work. I tried to do my job and no one from the company offered condolences or any sort of check in. I was left to hang in the wind. As long as the Pull Requests were complete, the Sprints were met, and the code I worked on was pushed to Production, I was left alone. But the guilt of losing my friends and the guilt of working for a team of monsters wore me down.

11

One Monday, after a breakfast consisting of eight shots of liquor, I arrived at work an hour late. I had a terrible nightmare that kept me awake all night. My dead friends were playing a card game together, at a table made out of Enlister parts. Their decaying bodies laughed and swayed as the cards kept falling apart. Clint kept asking Ramsey "where did you go, Rams?", then he would shake his head and laugh. And his voice grew louder every time.

Ramsey responded "I went where you went, Clint. I died!"

They laughed but it wasn't funny, it felt demonic. Clint grabbed Ramsey's hand and his arm fell off.

Ramsey turned to me and said "Look, no blood!"

Then he said, in a deep growl, "Jonas, do you know who killed us? Do you know Jonas?!" Clint joined in well and both were yelling "Do you know who killed us, Jonas?! Do you know who killed us, Jonas?! Do you know who killed us, Jonas?!"

I awoke, screaming, and jumped to my feet. I couldn't hold onto the guilt anymore, I had to do something. Even if I was an alcoholic loser at this point, I knew more about the code running the Enlisters than anyone else at my level. But I couldn't walk in and destroy everything. I had to spread dissent first and I chose to send a team-wide email once I got to my desk.

"Hello Team,

Happy fucking Monday, sorry I was late! I had a terrible dream featuring Ramsey and Clint. I decided to down several shots of liquor before coming into work. You all know that our company is responsible for their deaths? If not, you should get with the program. Speaking of programs, I think the world needs to learn more about what the fuck this company is up to, other than its financial reports. Money money money. Well not for long. More to come. See you in the break room!"

Later that day, the Director of my department called me into her office. She told me the email I had sent earlier was flagged by our IT Department and that I was on pace for a disciplinary action. She also said that further talk about what had happened to my friends, or voicing negative opinions about the company would set in motion something that was out of her control: a full on demotion to an Enlister Factory. The same factory where Clint had died.

"This isn't a threat, it's a fact, Jonas. You're a great employee, but it's obvious that your drinking has gotten out of control. Have you thought about having a dose of MORS technology injected to scrub your mind of the bad memories? It might improve your life." She asked.

"Lidia, I don't mean to be rude, but how old are you?" I asked her.

"Well, uh, I'm forty-seven, Jonas. Why does that matter?" She replied.

I asked her, "And what age did you receive your first Age Reversal injection?"

She said, "I was twenty-nine, right before my thirtieth birthday. It was a gift from my husband."

I responded, "OK, so don't you see the problem here? This company has granted you something people have been chasing for centuries and that is, infinite youth. Don't you view that as a conflict of interest?" She put her head down and rubbed her eyes.

I continued, "Say for example, your husband is murdered, and you know a faulty Enlister was responsible. Maybe he came to visit, was viewed as a threat, and was murdered right in front of you by mistake. Does it not worry you that the technology injected into your bloodstream could be used against you?"

I leaned back in my chair.

"Doesn't that ever cross your mind? This company has bought your compliance with youth and holds that over your head to make sure you never speak up if something goes awry."

She looked down at her desk and sighed. Then she lifted her head and told me, "Get the fuck out of my office. And if you ever pull some shit like you did today again, I'll make sure you're demoted before the end of the day. You'll become such a fixture at Rilekrin that the way out for you will be death. Do you understand?"

"Yeah, I get it, you don't fucking care. I'm heading home for the day. See you tomorrow, Lidia."

Before I left work, I pushed the latest source code for the Enlister software to a remote drive that I could access from outside the corporate network. I knew there were no backdoors in the software. But I could program them, push the code back to the repository, then update the signature through a manual command, thus erasing any proof that the code was accessed outside of the network or outside of business hours. I had a high level of clearance and CyberSynth would have no idea what was happening until it was too late.

Every night, I dissected the code, made notes of what sections needed to be analyzed, and outlined a potential back door. I executed test cases and watched them fail, one after the other. One evening, I realized I needed some Enlister parts in order to achieve a successful test case. That was the reason why the code would not execute on its own. It needed hardware components. I worked on the Development team for years and it never occurred to me. I stopped what I was doing and looked at the clock. It was dark outside and late enough in the day for the security at the factory to now be in shifts. Of course, CyberSynth had people working

24 hours a day, but the after hours crew was sparse compared to the day shift. The security patrol was other human beings, along with the typical Enlisters.

The Enlister software still wasn't smart enough to make informed decisions regarding life and use of excessive force. The company was forced to involve human personnel after several "incidents". It was never disclosed to the public what those incidents entailed, but most of us figured it had something to do with a group of high school students who were killed after skateboarding on the sidewalk outside the entrance to headquarters. The story didn't make national headlines and wasn't even much of anything on the local level. Money talks, or in this case, keeps people from talking. Either way, security was a mixed bag as far as Organic Machines and humans. Enlisters now alert their human counterparts instead of taking action and I would be able to get away if it wasn't working out like I expected. I had a vision of putting on a button down shirt, with a jacket and jeans, and my badge around my neck. I would go up to the security booth and make up a story. Tell them a surprise check in from higher up in the company; an audit on the new security measures. That fell apart in my head when I realized I didn't have a badge to hold my claim in place.

I would have to sneak into the factory and somehow steal the critical parts of an Enlister: the Operating System and a skull. The OS was stored within the chest of every Organic Machines on a device called a "HardHeart", like a hard drive and heart combination. And the "brain" holds the remaining components. Those parts are called "Frains", short for "fake brains". Very clever. The Frains and the HardHearts worked together, with cables running down the back of the neck, much like a spine. Heat played a major role in the overall functionality of an Enlister, and that's why each of them contained a fluid that looked like oil. In reality, it isn't oil, it's a proprietary substance used to cool the hardware. We used to say that Enlisters are cold-blooded and that's almost a literal fact. The company calls it "Boil Point". That has a tinge of irony attached to it since it does not boil. Stupid names aside, I would need a canister of Boil Point, a HardHeart, and a Frain. Lucky for me, all of those were kept on the same floor at the factory. Much to my chagrin, I didn't have an easy way into the factory.

CyberSynth has a multi-faceted business model, and the sourcing for the materials takes place on site near their factories. Urban development grew in the central and south Texas areas throughout the 2040's and that led to the discovery of a new element called "Kalnerite". Kalnerite was placed in all of the Organic Machines and was necessary for the operation of the artificial intelligence hardware and software combination. The drilling company was owned by Xavier Lambert, which facilitated an easy transition from proof of concept to full on Organic Machines that looked and sounded human. The corporate office that I worked in happened to be next to the original mining site that was still in use and the industrial lift was always open. Workers could move from the mine up to the factory floor and drop off supplies. The entryway to the mine was half a mile away from the factory but since it was a hazardous work zone and the electricity was limited, there were no security cameras within the mine. I threw on a sweatshirt and sweatpants, grabbed work gloves, a backpack, wire cutters, a hat, and a scarf to cover my face. I drove to the mine and parked a block away.

It was humid, misty. The area surrounding the mine was wooded so the front was visible from the street but the rest of the fencing was hidden behind the trees. I regretted wearing a sweatshirt since I could feel the beads of sweat precipitating on my back. Some of that was nerves, of course.

The fence looked to be about eight feet tall with thin coils of razor wire across the top. That's a lot harder to work around compared to barbed wire. There were plastic strips woven into the links of the fence for added privacy and to prevent people from climbing over. I took out the wire cutters, and managed to cut a hole wide enough to fit through. I covered my face with the scarf, put my gloves on, and crawled through the gate. It was not well lit but it was easy to see there were no security cameras. And the company relied upon physical security and their own CCTV system rather than Black Bird Cameras. They were too expensive to replace and since people were often unhappy, it was very easy to destroy them and there would be no trace as to who was responsible.

The door to the mine was unlocked and that led to an industrial elevator that took you straight down a vertical tunnel. It was too quiet and I wanted to get in and out, as fast as possible. A detour was out of the question. If I got caught here, the consequences would be dire as would the consequence of being caught stealing proprietary code. Once I was in the mine, I continued on the single pathway and followed the signs that pointed toward the factory elevator. The white lights lining the ceiling were dimmed and that acted as an additional barrier against someone finding me. The

line of sight visibility must have been five feet or
so. My experience felt divine- not much light, no
one was around, easy entry, almost no barriers. I felt
like I was being compelled by another force to bring
down this company.

I had arrived ten minutes before and I was
now entering the elevator to get to the factory floor.
Once I was in, I knew where to go thanks to the
many tours I had taken. I took the items I needed
and left quickly. Not a single soul, or Organic
Machine, could be found. My face was obscured
enough so that security footage would not be solid
enough to place blame on any one person. Plus, the
factory was producing Organic Machines at such a
high rate that inventory was not taken very often. I
jogged back through the mine, into the parking lot
and out of the hole in the fence; placing the cut
chain links back in place. If someone wasn't
looking for it, no one would ever notice the fence
had been cut. I got back in my car and made it back
to my apartment with no issues.

I spent a number of weeks running through
test cases. Once my work was complete, I had to
acquire a Continuum Resetter. That would be a little
more challenging to procure as not many people had
access to that kind of technology. Some C-level
executives had them, they had been given out as

awards during year-end celebrations. But not many people practiced Distancing. And none of those higher ups were bold enough to try it out. After all, you can't take a yacht with you. Besides that, It was still a new technology and with unknown side effects so I didn't blame them. Almost no humans had jumped back because we didn't know for certain that we could return to the present. Most of the experiments were done using Organic Machines. And not the Enlisters, those were too expensive. Instead, CyberSynth sent back smaller components, with built-in directives. Most of them buried themselves at certain latitude and longitude coordinates and were left to sit under the ground until recovery. I believe it started small, with one week, one month, one year, and so on.

The biggest breakthrough was when CyberSynth sent something back to 2014 and recovered the item. It showed some signs of decay and was no longer functional so it was apparent that it hadn't been faked. It made international headlines, and a lot of regulations were put in place to prevent the technology from being used without specific authorization. It was a way for CyberSynth and the US Government to maintain all rights and prevent competitors or other governments from stealing it and going back in time to do whatever they wanted. That was a move I agreed with, along with most of us that worked for the company. But the awards went out to the executives who helped patent the Continuum Resetters, with actual Continuum Resetters as the "trophy". At the ceremony, Xavier Lambert joked about how the recipients were too afraid to use them so it would be safe to dole them out. He wasn't wrong and even though the devices had an air of mystery surrounding them, instructions were provided so anyone could use a Continuum Resetter with little effort. One of the C-level executives who received the award was someone I was pretty familiar with. She was the Vice President of marketing, had a corner office on my floor, and was seldom in the office. It was on a shelf behind her desk on a small pedestal. It was out of plain sight and very easy to steal.

I waited until the end of the day on a Friday, when almost everyone on my floor had left. With a blank envelope in my hand, I walked into her office, dropped the blank envelope onto her desk, and put the Continuum Resetter in my bag and left. I did that so if anyone did happen to see me, it would look like I was returning mail and nothing more. And if she found the envelope, it wouldn't stick out. Once she even figured out the Continuum Resetter was gone, I would be decades in the past. Everything had been way too easy up to that point.

So it made sense that the following Monday, I was removed from my position and demoted to the factory, on a permanent basis.

I had two Enlisters show up at my door on Sunday and they demanded my company laptop. One of them delivered a message from upper management that read like a demented telegram.

"Hello Jonas. Due to your recent erratic behavior and your speaking out against the Company and its practices, you have been relieved of your duties as a Product Developer. You are now assigned to the Rilekrin Factory, located on Commerce Street. Considering you were the lead Product Developer and to thank you for your years of service, your pay will not be reduced. You are to now report to Rilekrin beginning tomorrow morning and you are no longer allowed to enter Headquarters without being accompanied by an Enlister or human equivalent. Failure to report to the factory will result in your immediate arrest and you will be placed in custody of the State for an indefinite sentence. Thank you for your understanding of this matter." It looked at me with a half-hearted attempt at a smile.

"Fuck you, you mindless piece of shit." I said.

"Thank you for your understanding of this matter." It handed me a transcript of the message it had recited.

I told them, "Get fucked, and get off of my property, now!"

It repeated, "Thank you for your understanding of this matter."

"You're welcome, message received, now, get the fuck out of here." I slammed the door as the two of them walked out.

I sat in silence at my table. It's not like I didn't see this coming, but it did sting a bit to be tossed out to a factory. The conditions were not ideal, no air conditioning, everyone was wearing rags or ventilators because of the smell. Most of the air in the city was horrible, except for in the Domes. At least my pay wasn't decreased so I wouldn't be forced to move. My apartment was in a Dome. And my plan could move forward. So, while the company felt it would be a detriment to kick me out of headquarters, in reality, it accelerated my motivation to bring it all down. I spent the next two months working with the stolen Continuum Resetter, testing it against the Organic Machines parts, and exposing the command prompt in order to write the Bash commands. I tested and retested, with a 100% success rate. Once that threshold had been reached, I set my operation in motion. With the Continuum Resetter in my bag, I set out for my final shift at the factory.

12

The tracking device Xavier mentioned during our confrontation was stored in the headliner of my car. I discovered that after I pulled off into a public rest and picnic area on the island. Since the ferry wasn't running until morning, that was the best option. When I climbed into the back seat, a small slit in the ceiling caught my eye, above the rear passenger door. Upon opening the slit, I found the tracking device, still active, a little blue light blinking on and off. I ripped it out, broke it, and tossed it into some brush. Xavier must have known I would find it, or maybe he didn't. It didn't feel advantageous for me to leave it there but removing it didn't seem to sway my thinking on that matter very much either. Damned if you do, damned if you don't. I never felt safe, no matter how many lengths I went to. At least I could sleep knowing the Enlisters would have difficulty finding me from that point forward.

I sat up from the back seat and looked out to see people moving in and out of their cars, coming and going to and from the bathroom and vending machines. I had forgotten that people enjoyed lakes and time with their families. I was no longer certain what day of the week it was. The last words Xavier spoke to me hung in my mind. "Think about it and we'll talk soon." What did that mean? Xavier knew something I didn't, and I was determined to find out what that was. Renata's mansion was compromised and going there would be a death sentence. He said "eyes everywhere", and I believed him.

I wanted to clean myself up a bit so I washed my face in the bathroom, and got back in my car. I drove for a few blocks and stopped at the Oasis Island Market. I grabbed a pack of bottled water and some food. I hadn't eaten in days and really needed to get that under control. I had grown accustomed to fasting but it wasn't like me to go this long without food. I paid for my groceries and on my way out to the car, I saw a stand of free newspapers sitting near the exit. On the front page, in big bold letters read the headline "**Fountain Research To Host Annual Employee Gathering At The Aragon Hote**l"

My mouth dried up, again. I snatched the newspaper off the stand and rushed back to my car. I skimmed through the article and saw that the party was happening on June 27th. I wanted to see if there were any archives about this event so I searched for *"Fountain Research Aragon Hotel June 27 2026"* and clicked on an article I found from *Local Business Today*:

Monday, June 29 2026

The Beauty Research and Anti-aging firm, Fountain Research, held an invitation only event at the Aragon Hotel. Billionaire investor and entrepreneur, Xavier Lambert, was in attendance. The event, billed as a 'Summer Night to Remember', served as an employee appreciation gathering but also doubled as the biggest night in the hotel's three year history.

"It was an outstanding event for our hotel and it is the first time we have ever been at full capacity" says Manager Natalie Wilson. "We believe that event will catapult The Aragon to the forefront of the tourism industry and will become the number one hotel destination for travelers who visit our city."

Indeed, the event seemed to be larger than life itself. Spotlights on the roof, red carpet entry, free valet service for all guests, open bar, and a discounted room rate for employees. But it wasn't the party that drew the attention of the public. Xavier Lambert's attendance was the main attraction. Known as a billionaire, an investor, entrepreneur, and CEO of Prism Security, Xavier Lambert is anything but an unknown name. With his dealings in the Middle East and secrecy surrounding his personal life to his involvement in shady business practices and investments, he has drawn the ire of many in the public and private sectors. Still, Lambert looks to expand his enterprise.

"We're looking at different ways to expand the Prism Security imprint and also dive into different markets." The CEO said. "Renata Caldwell (CEO of Fountain Research) and I have been great friends for a long while and are very interested in doing business together. Where that journey will take us is yet to be seen."

There has been speculation that the two are romantically involved, a rumor to which Renata Caldwell herself has disputed.

"Xavier and I are friends and have known each other for years, but we are nothing more than friends," she said.

Other business insiders have theorized that perhaps the two of them will merge their corporations or form a new business altogether considering Donovan White, CEO and Chief

Architect of Red Index, a developmental technology
company, and Ellis Murdoch, CEO and Chief
Architect of BionicShift, a robotics company, were
also in attendance. Time will tell what will become
of this 'meeting of the minds' but one thing is
certain, The Aragon Hotel is here to stay.

"It was a great night for our hotel and staff
and we welcome any and all corporate events!"
said Wilson."

The original article listed that Donovan and Ellis were there so that must mean that not every action I take has affected the future. Or CyberSynth corrected the timeline? Based on what I've heard from working for CyberSynth, the time travel "rules" we've learned from Science Fiction movies and books don't apply to real life. If something happens in the "past", the "future" timeline is unchanged unless someone dies. Death appears to be the permanent occurrence that will change things. And this of course is why the article mentioned Donovan and Ellis. Machines aren't human and don't affect the world in the same way, for whatever reason. They could have been rebuilt before the event mentioned in the paper. It didn't seem possible, Organic Machines underwent a long and tedious assembly process. But based on the way everything had gone up until now, I couldn't rule it out. I had to be prepared.

I scrolled down a little further in the search results and saw an invitation for the party. I printed that out and stuck it in the glove box.

Going in there with my rifle during the party wasn't an option, and that meant checking into a room had moved to the top of my priority list. I didn't have a proper ID and I assumed the Aragon wasn't going to put up with the "large amount of cash" option. I could wait until the 26th and force my way in, walk through the front door in a ski mask and demand the staff get on the floor, kick open the ball room door and go straight for Xavier. Fire a shotgun point blank in his chest, go after Renata, then be taken out by the swath of private security. Or I could check in days ahead, learn more about the layout, the exits, the main ballroom. Enter the party as a guest and lurk my way through the crowd. Find Renata and Xavier and kill them both. One of those scenarios sounded more entertaining but the other had better chances of a positive outcome. I stared off into space and went over what could happen. Before I even realized it, my car was in drive and I was heading to the Aragon hotel.

A valet was out front at a podium and there was a garage across the street. A valet sign on the wall read "$40 for 24 hrs." A man handed me a ticket, and took my keys. I walked up the concrete steps, entered through the revolving door and into the lobby.

There was a small cafe to the right and a bar in front of me, towards the back. There were a lot of people in business attire and I stuck out more than I would have liked to. I was like a rusty knife in a drawer full of expensive silverware. No one looked at me, and that was great, considering my clothes were dirty. Bribing my way into a room was not an option. This place would require some identification and a credit card, at least.

I sat in a tall chair near the end of the bar. I had a plan to glean as much information as I could while I was here. There were tables with comfortable lounge chairs throughout the space, occupied by different groups of people. The chatter was loud but not unbearable. The bartender came over to me and placed a napkin down. I ordered a drink, leaned on the bar, and looked around. At the opposite end of the bar, a woman in business attire with a name tag that had "MANAGER" written underneath her name on her left lapel approached the bar with a small stack of papers.

"Jim, here is the schedule for the party on Saturday. It covers the deliveries that will happen that morning, plus what to expect from the various vendors and security that will be on site." She handed one to the bartender and he held it in both of his hands and looked it over.

"OK, thank you, Natalie. I'll look this over and make sure the crew understands." He said as the manager turned and continued looking at the schedule.

He came back over to where I was seated and placed the paper behind the bar. I finished my drink sooner than I had planned and set the glass down. He looked up and offered me another. When he handed me my second drink, I decided to ask him about the upcoming event.

"Y'all having a party?" I said, as I took a sip and set my drink down.

"Yes, there is a big company in town having an event on Saturday. It's supposed to be a big deal for us. We're excited to finally use the ballroom!" He said.

"Oh, there's a ball room here?"

"Yeah, the wall behind me." He pointed behind the bar, "it's retractable and it opens up into a huge ballroom. We'll have an open bar here and another inside the ballroom."

"Are you earning some extra cash for that?"

"No, no, I'm staying away from that. I do not work on the weekends here. Save that for the young people." He said.

"Good call, I wouldn't want to get involved in that either." I said.

He must've been close to his mid-forties and slender, with some facial hair.

He replied, "Yes, sir, too many parties for me when I was a kid. I work the day shift here. We have a lot of clientele that are very… well off. So I don't need to work on the weekends."

"Yeah, I hear you. Well, thanks for the drink." I held it up toward him and pressed it to my lips.

"Yeah let me know if you need anything else!" He said.

I nodded my head and he took another drink order from someone else on the other side. It was good to know he wouldn't be here on Saturday, one less face to recognize me. I looked over at the schedule that he had set down not too far away. The font was small and I couldn't read much. But from what I gathered, caterers would arrive at 4 PM and the party commenced at 7 PM. A three hour block to get in here before everyone arrived. I might be able to somehow sneak in with the catering group or another person involved in the setup. I took another sip of my drink and looked into the bottom of the glass. Then I ordered a second, followed by a third.

My mind slipped in and out of doubt, certainty, fear, bravery. I was under the impression this would be the last place I would be seen alive. I had a plan to invade a hornet's nest and Xavier had to be plotting for my arrival. I wished I could stay in there, lay low out in the open. The money I could print looked real. I'm sure I could find a template for a driver's license and it would look authentic. But that wouldn't be enough. The staff at this hotel would want a Credit Card, and that wasn't something I could produce. I needed to hide and wait. I turned my head around and broke my trance. The conclusion to my thoughts walked away. The next step hung up the phone without saying goodbye. Stuck again, zoned out.

Fear crept in, then out again, and I shifted back over to bravery. I was sure of myself one minute, doubting everything within another minute. I needed to get out of there. I got up from my seat and left some cash near my empty glass. I needed new clothes, I needed to shower. I needed sleep. I still wasn't sure about the day of the week. I knew that Saturday was coming up, but was it Tuesday? Was it Thursday?

"Hey, thanks for the tip, my friend!" The bartender said, shaking me out of my trance.

"Anytime! Will you be working tomorrow?" I asked.

"No, sir. I am not here on the weekends." He said.

"Oh right, sorry, it's Friday, it's been a long week!" I said.

"No problem! Enjoy your night!" He gave a quick wave and I left.

At least I had an answer to my question. It's Friday, the day before the event. That left me with no time to prepare. Then I remembered how I had even zeroed in on this hotel. The invitation I received this morning gave me admittance into the party. I don't know how I forgot that. My mind was wrecked. I needed to clean myself up.

A valet was out front and I gave him my ticket. Another cheap place to stay was in my future. An evening filled with counting bullets, fighting sleep, followed by trying to sleep. Out of my mind in every possible way.

13

I found a cheap motel not too far from The Aragon. I ran through the same song and dance with the clerk up front, got my key, went back outside and opened my trunk.

I gathered my weapons then rushed to the door to my room. I threw it open, forced it shut, then deadbolted it. My plan for tomorrow evening and how everything could go was in the forefront of my mind. I sat in a chair next to a table across from the bed. Everything felt so heavy and so unimportant at once. What I wanted to do did seem impractical, in particular, trying to stop Xavier. His reach was endless, his Drones deployed across the city, Enlisters on his side, everywhere. I was coming to find out the technology was older than I knew. Or CyberSynth had sent back dozens to track me down, and Xavier knew that and was a willing counterpart to the overarching plan.

That didn't matter, though. If I got the chance to off Xavier again, I would not hesitate. I thought about the Suicide Bombers I had seen on the news growing up. I'm sure I could fashion explosives, strap them to my chest, go to The Aragon, straight up to Xavier, and detonate. That tactic did cross my mind. But as soon as that thought arrived, another pushed it aside. A government bent on controlling its citizens would leap at the chance to blame the death of these evil people on terrorists. They would restrict the public, prevent air travel, and lock down the city. I could see that happening anyway. But I didn't want to terrorize anyone, as much as I would sacrifice my own life. I should have fired as many rounds as possible at Xavier during our confrontation. I don't know why I froze, but I did, and it was wearing on me. If he were dead now, I would have the upper hand instead of being trapped in my position. If I go into that party and do anything in front of the public, it would be labeled as another "mass shooting", with people crying outside the hotel, phoning their loved ones.

"Fuck that, I can't do that. I'm better than that." I paced around the room and shut off my inner monologue.

"Fuck the party, fuck the hotel, I'm going for recon and that's it. I'll tail his ass, follow him home, blow up Renata's house, whatever it takes. But I'm not doing a damn thing at The Aragon. I can't do that. I'm better than that. I can't do that, I'm better than that."

My inner monologue didn't stay silent for long. I should go to the party and blend in, no, I should avoid it altogether. If I go, I could get captured, if I stay, I could get captured. The path that I am on has an inevitable conclusion and I doubt that would involve me being whisked away on the shoulders of a crowd cheering my name. If I survived, I would be surprised. I distilled my next steps down to this: I have nothing to lose. And nothing better to do. Might as well walk into the nest and lock eyes with the Devil himself. He wants me dead, but he can't have a publicized bloodbath. That will all but destroy his image and his plans for his company to merge with the partners.

I have no fear of death and no fear of Xavier. My attendance is unexpected, he'll be caught by surprise. Not unarmed but not ready for a fight either. I reviewed my small arsenal splayed on the bed. My rifle would remain in the trunk. Loaded, with a backup magazine next to it, and the safety on. I don't want to leave my car with the Valet so I will have to find parking elsewhere. I'll carry the Control Baton in my pocket, and keep my handgun on me as well. I still had bullets for both guns and I had a second clip for my pistol that I would keep on me as well. And I would have to put together some type of formal wear outfit so I could blend in with everyone. Did the invitation specify a dress code? I picked up the invitation off the dresser and re-read the text.

"…Casual Attire Welcome"

I knew from my previous corporate life that some people would wear suits and dresses and others would have jeans with boots. That was perfect for me. Carrying weapons and not standing out was a win-win. And I wouldn't have to buy a costume to look like a C-level executive to get into a fire fight with a bunch of Organic Machines. Win-win-win. I was hoping it wouldn't come to that, though. The thought of innocent casualties made me feel sick to my stomach. And I still needed new clothes. A shoulder holster, like the ones cops wear in movies. I also needed a suit jacket with extra pockets so I could bring an extra clip. Dead of summer or not, it's important. I pulled up my Continuum Resetter and found a clothing store not too far away. The hours were listed as 8 AM - 10 PM Central. It was 8:30 so I still had some time to get that out of the way tonight. A smaller crowd is always preferred. Call it paranoia or not wanting to interact with too many people. I grabbed my bag and started counting the money I had printed. I also checked the raw materials in my AM Machine and still had plenty left. I printed out thousands of dollars more and took it all with me.

I arrived at the clothing store and couldn't stop thinking about the staff being made up of Enlisters. Somehow, CyberSynth knew I would be here. I almost didn't get out of the car. Enlisters are coming. Enlisters are coming. Enlisters are already here.

"Stop!" My voice was so loud it bounced off the roof.

I had to snap myself out of it. Even if there were Enlisters here, I've stopped them before, I can stop them again. My hands wouldn't stop shaking as I grabbed the Control Baton with the keys in my hand. Breath entered my lungs through my nose and escaped through my mouth. I repeated that before opening the door. I glanced at my reflection in the rearview mirror, my eyes were bloodshot and tired. My skin was grimey. I realized I hadn't even showered since... before I left? I couldn't remember. Tomorrow will be better. My head wouldn't be spinning. Enlisters are coming. Right to my door. Waiting for me. Sitting on my bed. Standing, in sleep mode. Behind the door, within arms length. Close enough to grab me, far enough for the door to open all the way.

A mannequin staged in swimming attire was positioned near the front of the clothing store. I envisioned a world with fun, excitement, and water. I imagined a woman coming in, looking at the bathing suite, trying it on with her friend. Planning a fun vacation. Not knowing what the future held, not caring, in that moment. Happy to be out living her life. Being normal. Not even knowing that one day she would either be forced to live in compliance with the union between government and business. Or it would be her children. Or grandchildren. The confusion I understood as a part of Distancing was more ever present as I ran through this imaginary scenario than ever before. Trying to remember what year I had left, and what year this imaginary woman would face the dilemma I had strived to stop was hazy.

Enlisters are coming, Enlisters are in your hotel.

"I've got to get this shit out of my head."

My attention broke away from the mannequin standing as a silent ringmaster in my wild but benign scenario and turned toward the convenience store in the same parking lot.

"Fuck it."

A young guy sat on a stool, staring at his phone behind the register. I nodded when he looked up and as soon as that happened, he was looking down again. In the back of the store, I pulled a six pack out of the cooler. When I turned around, a man barged in, looking even worse than I did.

"Yo, Phillip, there was this dude today, he had metal hands. I seen him running around. I yelled at him, I said 'hey man, you got metal on your hands!' And he didn't even flinch. I couldn't believe it!" He pretty much shouted at the clerk.

The clerk, Philip, I presumed, looked up from his phone and entertained the man's story.

"Oh yeah, Richie? Where was this at?" He asked.

"Down the road man, like an hour ago. He talked to me and was like 'where is Jonas?' And I was like 'whatchu mean, 'where's Jonas? I don't know nobody named Jonas'" Richie said.

My mouth dried up, my pulse pounded in my teeth.

"He looked at me, real crazy, right, and said 'if you see Jonas, tell him I'm coming for him.' I said 'Yo, I ain't no snitch, bro, you gonna have to find Jonas your damn self.' He looked at me and like, kept on going. It was fucked up." Richie said with his eyes wide.

"Yeah, sounds like it, and you so happened to come here and tell me?" Philip asked.

"Shit man, you was the first person I wanted to tell when I was like 'oh hell, I gotta tell somebody!'"

Richie walked over to the rectangular cooler filled with ice and picked a tall boy. He kept talking with the clerk but I stopped paying attention. I hurried to the counter before he could and paid. Back in my car, I waited for him to walk out. I assumed he was homeless but couldn't tell for sure. He continued talking with the clerk for another minute or so then pushed the glass door open and drank his beer as he went down the sidewalk. I studied him as he continued. He moved in a brisk manner, like he was heading somewhere. He drank his one hand and scrolled through his phone with the other. I couldn't tell if he was a vagrant with a burner phone or a strange guy with an outgoing disposition. If he was chatty with the cashier then he would be chatty when I approached him. People that talk to strangers at a store may be full of all kinds of surprises. Would he engage me in a casual conversation about the guy with metal hands or would he try to fight me if I told him my name was Jonas? He seemed a little on edge, but so was I. My curiosity compelled me to open my mouth before he could cross into the intersection.

"Hey, Richie, can I talk to you for a second?" He had a look of confusion on his face. I jogged over to him.

"Yeah, hey, I heard you talking to that guy in the gas station. That's a crazy story. What do you think was going on with that?"

In an instant, his expression shifted.

"Yeah, it was weird as fuck! I was like 'is this dude for real?' Looked like a damn costume."

I laughed. "That is weird, can you tell me where that was? I want to see if I can find him."

Richie pointed to the intersection.

"It was two blocks back that way, down Lincoln. He's a big motherfucker, you can't miss him, if he's still there." He motioned with his hand and indicated the man he saw was a lot taller than he was.

"OK, cool, thanks, Richie."

"Yes sir!" He took a sip of his beer and went over to the cross walk, and looked at his phone again. I headed to Lincoln Avenue.

I pulled onto Halifax Drive and stopped at the next light. The rectangular, green and white "Lincoln Ave" sign swayed in the wind just up ahead. Something caught my attention out of my peripherals. A large figure moved down the street at a very fast pace, almost faster than a human could go, in my direction. It was the X1Y Enlister I was searching for except it was even bigger than the others. And CyberSynth had made no attempt to make it appear like a real person. Unlike the other Enlisters, this one was monstrous in every way. Pale-gray skin, stark metal hands, huge, bulky muscles, and a brow that formed a menacing scowl. It must have been 6 feet, 5 inches or taller. It wore green, military style pants with combat boots and a sleeveless black hoodie; the hood draped over the top of its head like the Grim Reaper. It was like a mad scientist's life's work. If intimidation was the goal, CyberSynth succeeded and terror coursed through my veins. People stopped to look as it marched down the street. I knew a confrontation was imminent. This Enlister was on a kill mission. As he got closer, my heart pounded and I held my gaze at the stop light. I was not about to get out and this thing. Not without a rifle in my hand. And not in front of all these people.

As he emerged from the nearest intersection, he didn't seem any more focused on my car or my direction than he was before. I saw his face but shot my eyes back at the stop light. I fixated on the glowing red circle and hoped he wouldn't see me. I didn't know how he had gotten this close to begin with; there must have been some type of surveillance. Something more than Black Birds or drones. Or another tracking device buried in my car. I tightened my hands on the steering wheel. Right then, the X1Y "Super" Enlister made himself visible in my field of vision. He lowered his head and ran towards me at full speed. His movements were fluid and furious, like a raging flood. And the gates had opened.

1 4

    I pressed my foot on the gas as hard as I could, peeled out of the intersection, and missed the Super Enlister by inches. His hands were outstretched as he reached for the hood of my car. In the rearview mirror, I saw him in a cloud of smoke. He looked a bit confused, whipping his head from side to side, until he saw my car speeding off ahead of him. He re-focused and charged after me. He must have been moving at 30 MPH, at least, and getting faster. With each step, he gained more and more ground. I kept my foot on the gas and my eyes on the next light. Still green, I sped through that intersection, changed lanes once, then back again, with the Super Enlister very close behind me. I weaved in and out of traffic and he mimicked my movement. I dodged left, he shifted left. I went back to the right and he did the same. I hit my breaks and expected to crash into him. He leapt to the side and landed against a pickup truck. He rolled onto the ground and back onto his feet like nothing happened. Other drivers laid on their horns as I careened through another intersection and fish-tailed onto Lincoln. With four lanes and a median separating traffic, Lincoln was almost empty. I looked back in my mirrors and saw pandemonium unfolding in his wake. He ran into another car, that driver lost control and collided into a light pole. Then another two cars slammed into that one. That didn't slow him down either. He was now halfway down the street, and getting even closer to my rear bumper.

Lincoln Avenue led straight to Highway 265. Once I got up to 65 MPH, he began to trail. I had a vision of being stopped at the on ramp, smelling like alcohol, with more beer, being asked where I was going, where I came from, stumbling over my words, stumbling out of the car, and stumbling into the back seat of a police cruiser so I slowed back down to the speed limit. I coasted to 55 MPH, took the exit for 265 and traveled back to my room. Both of my hands were white from how tightly they were gripping the steering wheel. That was CyberSynth' biggest, baddest weapon, the feeling I had in my throat was confirmation. They had nothing better than that, other than the sheer number of the criminals willing to pull a trigger for money. CyberSynth threw all they had in my direction, piece by piece. And that Super Enlister was still out there. I knew he would come looking for me. One way or another, our paths would cross again.

I kept on 265 for a bit before circling back to my hotel. Once I got there, I was so wound up that I "slept" facing the door, holding my rifle all night. Half-dreaming of being strangled by that mutant. When I awoke, I sat and stared at the back of the door, the morning sunlight seeped through the edges of the curtains. If that Enlister could run as fast as that, and it had a general idea of where I was, why didn't it kick my door down in the middle of the night? Couldn't CyberSynth just find me and kill me in my sleep? The constant eluding never felt like luck, it felt like it was part of the plan. And that always made my stomach feel like a bottomless pit. I got away *this* time, but what about next time? I sat up, set down my rifle and rubbed my eyes with my hands. I looked around the room and saw the alarm clock read 10:43 AM. I guess I had slept harder than I realized. I rolled out of bed and over to the curtains. There were puddles on the ground and water on the tops of some of the cars. Tonight was The Party and the forecast didn't care. A severe storm was not outside the realm of possibility. Still though, even if it was before noon, days tend to slip away from me and I wanted to be prepared. The clothing store was my first destination.

The metal handle on the door to the entrance felt cold, the condensation on the windows fogged up the bottom of the ground-to-ceiling glass walls. In the store, I could hear nondescript pop songs playing overhead. No one spoke to me but that was to be expected since it was a busy Saturday morning.

I scanned the store from the entryway and saw a sign that said *"MENS"* hanging from the ceiling. I walked to the section and passed a mirror along the way. I stopped and took a look at myself. I had bags under my eyes, my clothes were dirty. Self care and hygiene had taken a back seat since I had bought my current outfit from that thrift store.

I started in the dress pants but didn't stay there long. I was not "dressing to impress" and nothing would make me feel quite as dumb as carrying a gun in the pocket of a pair of nylon slacks. Plus, that type of material always made my skin crawl. No, I wanted another pair of black jeans. Form fitting, boring and unnoticeable. The one compromise to my attire would be the suit jacket. And new shoes. I couldn't go into The Aragon with my ordinary sneakers. As much as I figured people wouldn't notice, wearing that may come off as a fashion statement to someone that I'm not paying attention to; and small talk was not anything I could entertain. As I continued down the aisle, a young woman greeted me with a smile.

"Hi there, are you finding everything you're looking for?" She asked.

"Yes, I am, thanks." I said with a smile in return, as if I wasn't purchasing my casket outfit.

"You bet, hon. My name's Amber, let me know if you need anything!"

She smiled again and her heels clicked on the tile floor as she walked in the opposite direction. I looked back down at the jeans and something by the ceiling caught my eye. It was a camera. I saw at least three other cameras around the store. Anti-theft, I'm sure, but it was a reminder of what I was doing in this store to begin with. For a short moment, I had almost forgotten and felt like another patron shopping for clothes on a rainy Saturday. Cameras weren't always bad, in my opinion, and I understood their purpose, but the idea that if you aren't doing anything wrong, you shouldn't have anything to worry about, is the battle cry of a compliant-for-no-reason personality type. People who wish to forfeit their right to privacy for the idea that they themselves are not doing anything wrong are too afraid to stand up to authority. Or too afraid to assume a stance on a social issue that might rub someone the wrong way. In 2026, cameras in a clothing store were normal. But after a while, the concern for privacy gave way to the concern for safety, and so, more and more people, without much of a fight, relinquished their rights. And, thanks to technology, in my present-day, we had cameras that looked like bugs and birds fluttering around all over the world watching everything we were doing. All of this, while looking over a rack of black jeans, deciding which pair to purchase. I guess the philosophical idea of government or corporate overreach tends to creep up on a person like me.

I always felt responsible, even in a partial sense. And here I was, in the past, with a chance to stop it all, feeling compelled to pull out my pistol and shoot every camera in sight. I wanted to divulge my plan to anyone who would listen. Spread what I knew in hopes that strength in numbers would prevail. If everyone knew what would happen, we could put a halt to everything, together. But that was wishful thinking. One word of this to the general public and I could end up in a mental hospital. Trapped for the rest of my life. I pictured myself offering an explanation to doctors, calling out every major world event before it took place. And I would gain my freedom back, little by little. With each ear I turned, I would be one step closer to getting out and being back on track. But that sounded almost as bad as living in the future. Being confined to a mental hospital, living life as a subject of poking and prodding and question after question, sounded less and less appealing by the second. Best to shut up and pick out the clothes I wanted. Most people don't want to take a stand against anything, and I don't place blame, people are trying to live and be happy, but I couldn't sleep well at night going along with it all. And people in the past were no different than people in the future. So speaking out, even to someone I didn't know, was out of the question.

I found the pair of pants I wanted so I decided to check out the button downs. I chose to go with something a little more sophisticated than a black shirt so I picked out a black long sleeve dress shirt. Very original. Once I found that I moved onto the jackets: gray, red, brown, blue, purple, and of course, black. I toyed with the idea of wearing a red or purple jacket. Black or gray was more inconspicuous, so was the brown and blue. But the purple with a black shirt, pants, and shoes, it looked like it fit better. It wasn't an in-your-face, bright purple, but a more subtle color. The fact that I was contemplating it was enough for me to at least try it on. At the dressing rooms, the woman who had spoken to me earlier came over with keys.

"How many items?"

I counted them and said, "Uhh, looks like five."

"OK, five items." She grabbed a number five and hung it on the hook on the outside of the door.

"You can leave whatever you don't want hanging in the dressing room." She opened the door for me and walked off. In the mirror, the circles were even more apparent under the fluorescent lights. I'm surprised the woman working here was even the slightest bit polite. With my appearance she could have called security and had me escorted out. I put on the shirt and pants, followed by the jackets. All three of them fit well, each of them complimented the rest of the outfit the way I was expecting. The purple one did look a bit goofy but unexpected. And it fit a little nicer over my wrists. The other two covered my hands more than what I preferred. I took a step back and looked at myself in the mirror. It had been so long since I had worn what I thought of as fancy clothing. I couldn't even remember when I last had on something other than jeans and a t-shirt. The purple jacket was a decent look. It was subtle enough so I decided to go with it. I left the unwanted items hanging in the dressing room and continued onto the shoe selection. The shoes were located in a separate room, almost like a separate store altogether. There were dress shoes along the back wall, boots on the left wall, rows of athletic and casual shoes in the middle of the store.

And children's shoes as well. Unlike the clothing section, there weren't many people on this side.

A man in dress clothes approached me from behind and said, "Hey, how are you doing today? Is there anything I can help you find?"

How could I say that I wanted dress shoes with steel toes that I could also run in? I was under the impression those didn't exist so I opted for a more neutral response.

"Yeah, I need something to go with this outfit." I held up the clothes I had picked out.

He looked them over and pointed to the back of the store and led me in that direction.

"I think you'll find something over here that will match. Do you have a color in mind?" He asked.

"Black, if possible. And I want a pair that's comfortable." I said.

"Of course, I know how stiff these can be sometimes. What's the occasion, if you don't mind me asking?"

Suicide mission or total annihilation of an evil corporation were inappropriate answers so I said, "Company party this evening."

"Great, I think I have some items that may interest you. Do you have a specific budget?"

"No, I'm open to whatever prices you have. I just want something that fits."

"Gotcha, well these up here are the highest quality and are on the top end as far as price. The ones in the middle are a little more affordable, but you do sacrifice some quality. And the bottom ones I wouldn't buy."

He and I both laughed and he said, "Anyway, let me know if you want to try anything on."

"Sure, thank you."

Almost right away, my eyes landed on a pair of loafers. No laces was a good idea. Less interference and the insoles were padded. I set them back down and overlooked the section. The shoes were nice but not what I was looking for. I didn't want to go in expecting a fight wearing shoes that looked like I was at a wedding. I wanted something that I could kick with once the inevitable moment arrived when I would have to kick something. As my eyes wandered around the store, I found a pair of lace up boots on the left wall. A yellow tag that said "steal toe" was hanging off of the top of one of the boots. I held up the pants to the boots and it looked like a match. I picked one up and called out the clerk.

"Hey, do you have these in a size 10?"

The clerk headed over and took the boot from me.

"Hmm, I should. Are you opting for boots instead?" He asked.

"Yeah, I've been looking for boots like this and I figured I might as well get something that I can wear more than once." I said.

"Sure, no problem, let me see what I can find." He walked off to the back.

A moment or so passed and I looked over to see a man in the other half of the store, staring at me. I looked back at him and placed my hand on the collapsed Control Baton in my back pocket. Who is this guy? Is that another Enlister? Someone who works for Xavier? How do CyberSynth always know where I am? As I started to step in his direction, he shot a passive smile and averted his attention over to his family. I realized that he wasn't even looking at me, he was looking at the giant "15% OFF" sign hanging above my head. Paranoia runs deep and there was little I could do to stifle that. I still felt like an idiot, though.

The clerk returned with a pair of boots and I tried them on.

"These are steel toe, waterproof upper, with a teflon composite with makes them pretty hardy. And lighter than traditional leather boots." He said.

"Yeah, these are great, I'll take them." I took them off and handed him the box.

"OK, sounds good, I'll take these to the register. Do you want to check out here or are you still shopping?"

"I think I'm all set."

"Alright, I can get you right over here." He pointed toward the register, "Will that be cash or card, Jonas?"

"I'm sorry, what was that?"

"Cash or card?"

I was hearing things again. Or was I?

"Oh, uhh, cash please."

He scanned all of the items and put them in a large bag.

"We have a 15% off sale happening this weekend so your total comes out to $294.44"

I pulled out some cash from my pocket and counted out three hundred.

He handed me my change, placed the shoes and clothes in a bag, and handed that over as well. I thanked him and hurried out of the store. I couldn't get over the fact that I heard him say my name. Or he didn't say my name. Lack of good sleep and overall fear was playing a part there. Did he really say my name?

One the drive back, I kept going over what happened. His voice replayed so much in my head that I didn't know for sure what he said anymore. I was sleep deprived, I could not think straight, no matter how hard I tried. I threw open the door to my room and let it slam behind me. I shoved as much furniture as possible in front of it, blocking or at least slowing down any potential intruders. I set my things down on the table, fell onto the bed, and was asleep in less than a minute.

I awoke hours later and the room had been rearranged, with some of the furniture missing. It was dark outside but somehow still well lit. I got out of bed and looked for my gun, thinking someone might be in the room. It was gone and all of my belongings had vanished. In a panic, I tried to run, but my legs weighed a ton. It took all of my strength to take a couple of steps. Once I made it to the door, I opened it and stepped out into a large building. There were rooms everywhere with light coming from the ceiling. Nothing seemed familiar. I wandered down the main hallway, looking around from left to right. At the end, I found the front desk of the hotel, except it was different. It had a huge panel across the top that looked like a motherboard and it floated above the ground. A stripped down Organic Machine sat where a clerk would be, in front of a dark red wall. Its skin was pale white with no hair or eyebrows. It smiled and I heard a voice but its mouth didn't move.

Something said to me, "Welcome to the Aragon Hotel, sir. Please enjoy your stay."

It pointed to a wall that was now opening. Another room appeared in front of me, with a green glow. Thick fog poured out and I said, "I'm not going in there." My voice was muffled. I tried to scream and nothing came out.

With its eyes now holes in its head, and oil spilling out of its mouth, it shouted in a demonic and distorted voice "Of course not!"

The Organic Machine pointed its thin, mechanical finger at my face. I felt something poking against my teeth. I stuck my hands up to my cheek. I reached my fingers into my mouth and grabbed a hold of something moving like a snake. I pulled as hard as I could and out came a worm made out of machine parts. The Organic Machines looked at me and grabbed my arm. Its eyes were glowing now and the oil had dried up.

It said to me in a quiet voice, "don't you see that we can hear? Do you know that we can know?"

It pushed me and I fell back.

My eyes shot open.

I sat up in my bed and pressed my hand onto my cheek. I scrambled into the bathroom and switched the light on. I inspected my cheek, my gums, my teeth, my entire mouth. It was a dream. I turned the sink on and splashed water on my face. I was relieved to see the room hadn't changed; Everything was where I left it. A real sense of relief washed over me. Something I had not experienced since arriving in 2026. The clock read 7 PM so I took that as a sign to put on the last outfit I may ever wear and head to the Aragon.

1 5

While driving to the event, it occurred to me, yet again, that I had no visitors at my hotel. The uncertainty of whether I was outsmarting Xavier or if he was outsmarting me was unnerving. I was almost comfortable facing them all head on. As comfortable as could be, given the circumstance. I knew that Renata would be there, as well as Xavier, and his private security. Though, I did not expect anything significant to happen. That wasn't what I wanted to happen, at least.

The road was blocked as I approached a line of cars leading to the Aragon. A man in a Prism Security uniform checked each guest, as they handed over their invitations. When my turn arrived, I did the same. The guard glanced at my invitation and waved me through. There were signs pointing towards valet or self parking, with traffic being diverted by more Prism Security. Most other cars chose valet, and I searched for a place to park in the garage across the street. It was packed throughout so I ended up on the roof with no other cars around. The Aragon was massive, towering well above the six story parking garage. Over the edge, I could see people dressed in elegance going in through the entrance that was complete with a red carpet. It looked like an award ceremony for pompous celebrities, and it took a quick reminder to myself that the attendees were, in-fact, employees, and not wealthy elitists. I was there to gather intel and show my face to Xavier. And if he was anything like he was in the future, he would be roaming about the party, making sure everyone knew he was present.

Flashes of my deceased friend, my parents who had died too young, people suffering in the factories, filled my mind. I bowed my head with my eyes shut. I thought about protection of the innocent and guidance. I thought about doing what was right, even if it meant death.

I said aloud, "Righteous anger" and the words bounced off of my skull and rocked around in between my ears. A sense of peace overcame me as the wind blew and chills rolled across my body. I lifted my head and let the air fill my lungs. I exhaled and walked to the elevators.

On the ride down, my neck was pulsating with anxiety. The peaceful feeling I had on the rooftop had been dethroned by that feeling of dread, my oldest companion. After descending multiple floors, the elevator stopped, and the doors opened. A somewhat tall, slender woman with high cheekbones and blue eyes, stood at the opening.

Two men dressed in suits with ear pieces accompanied her on both sides. It was clear that she had undergone surgeries to keep her appearance young, even if it had the opposite effect. Her perfume engulfed my nostrils and I stopped myself from reacting. She was ugly, though not in the typical sense of the word. Her faded beauty had been propped up with a facelift here, a lip injection there, and caked on make-up, like plastic coming to life.

I could feel the guilt in the air, but not guilt as in regret, it was not her conscience speaking out. Rather the guilt of crimes against humanity. The slamming of a gavel after a judge sentenced a brutal killer to death. A killer who smiled at his victims' families in the courtroom. It almost seeped out of her skin and hung in the air the way her perfume did. She was a vile person, and it was apparent to anyone with even a shred of morality.

To her credit, she looked the same now as she did in the future. If someone had told me she slept in embalming fluid, I would have believed them. Her ultimate goal in life was to live forever and she had at least done well enough to preserve her face and her figure for that matter.

I had tried to find her mansion, I had been hunting her down, but Renata Caldwell had escaped every conflict; unbeknownst to herself. Yet here she was, right in front of me. My hands were tingling again.

The doors opened on the ground floor and I waited for a moment to create space between myself and them. Once they had taken several steps, I started walking too and ended up passing them on the way to the entrance. I didn't even want to look at her, truth be told, I couldn't look anywhere else but straight ahead. My teeth were clenched, my palms were sweaty, and I was locked in. So much so that I ignored the final Security check. A man ran out in front of me and guided me back to the doors. I lifted my arms and he scanned my torso and legs with a hand-held metal detector. I apologized and entered the lobby of the Aragon Hotel.

Security had the party separated with red velvet ropes and gold plated posts. You could feel a sense of tension from the Prism Security guards themselves. Each of them throughout the venue, holding walkie-talkies, and looking around, their movements bordered on erratic. The target was in their midst but cluelessness abounded. And I continued to wonder why that was. I felt like I had done a sloppy job, and it was odd for the authorities to be that far behind. But alas, I was here, making my way into the ballroom with no one stopping me at the door. A slowdown took place outside of the ballroom. Guests congregated and took photos. They were all amused at something, but it was hard to make out what it was.

As the crowd cleared, I saw what had captivated everyone's attention. A pale and hairless, Organic Machine was placed outside of the ropes in front of the ballroom. A man was there beside it, speaking and answering questions from intrigued guests. He said it was a prototype and was a product of years of development at BionicShift. He also said it knew some phrases and would speak if spoken to, but that BionicShift was a long way off from implementing what the company referred to as a "think for itself" model. That was a lie, considering Donovan White and Ellis Murdoch were both Organic Machines. But this guy didn't know he was lying, for all he knew, the technology was decades away from doing what BionicShift hoped it could do.

The Organic Machine was almost an exact match to what was in my dream and a memory I had long forgotten came flooding back: we had these in a storage room at the CyberSynth headquarters and we used to study them when we were in the developmental phase. Or we would set them up when we were bored and have them repeat funny phrases to make each other laugh. I hadn't thought about that in years. And we learned from notes in the code that the original Engineers had programmed a "verbal shutdown command". That was removed from later versions of the Organic Machines once CyberSynth determined their use would be dedicated to replacing human security. It wouldn't make for a successful Enlister if you could mutter a phrase and have it shut itself down. I continued on and before I entered the ballroom, I looked at the Organic Machine.

The man tending to it, laughed with other guests and said to me, "Go ahead, say something and end it with 'repeat back' and it will say it back to you! Keep it clean, of course!"

Without much of a pause, I said "Over the rainbow played in reverse unlocks the secrets of the universe."

Its glowing eyes went dark and it shut down. There would be no more demonstrations, or cutesy, word-repeating for the party guests. Now, it was a useless piece of synthetic materials, weighing somewhere around two hundred pounds. In the way more than anything else.

"Hey, what… what happened? What did you say?!" The man said. He was no longer looking at me and had become fixated on trying to get it to wake back up. He was joined by other staff members who were confused as well. The crowd that had amassed behind me was in full dissipation and the line moved again, faster than before. I laughed to myself, while people struggled to move the Organic Machine off to the side.

Once in the massive ballroom, I beelined to a seat at an empty table with an electronic candle placed in the middle. All of the tables had this feature, along with white tablecloths and silverware wrapped in cloth napkins. Fog from a machine near the DJ was adrift and multi-colored lights shined on the dance floor. Even still, it was very dim. Makeshift drink stations were scattered around the ballroom, as well as wait staff moving throughout the party. I saw that Renata was also there, still with her security. She was socializing with other guests, not a care in the world. I wondered if she was even real, or if she was a machine too. Did she know that I tried to kill her? People like Renata tend to think that invincibility is a skill you can attain with massive amounts of money. And people around her think that keeping someone safe is by keeping information from them. The CEO of a major, or even minor, corporation doesn't know that the faucet in a bathroom on the bottom floor is leaking. I'd like to think of myself as more than a leaky faucet, but I'm sure the people around her felt I was only a drop of water due to be dried with a single ply of cheap tissue paper. Thus there would be no need to explain to her that a man from the future stole a yet-to-be-invented time traveling technology, and came back to kill her and her colleagues.

As I continued staring, my attention was averted to someone else staring at me. It was another security guard, he also had an earpiece and was in an outfit that matched the body guards next to Renata Caldwell. While maintaining eye contact, he lifted his hand and spoke into the cuff of his sport coat. He walked off and I couldn't see him any longer. I waited for a group of security guards to approach me but no one ever showed up. I ordered a drink from a waitress and waited. Still nothing happened. I blended in well, even if I was alone, and the security guard I made eye contact with was employing an intimidation tactic.

I ordered a drink from the wait staff, and after it was brought to me, I decided to meander. The room was now filled with at least a hundred people, maybe more. I wanted to confront Xavier or, at a minimum, have a conversation with him. I wanted him to know that I was here. My stroll escalated from casual to quick as I scanned the crowd. On the far side of the room, outside of the crowd, was a large, conference style table. And there, sat Xavier, along with Renata and their security teams. And some other people I didn't recognize. Company high-rollers, more C-level executives.

I approached the table and pulled out a chair. "Is this seat taken?"

I set my glass on the table and stared right at Xavier, his mouth open as he was in the middle of a sentence. He was surprised and his security team got up from their chairs, but Xavier waved them off. "No, no it's fine guys, have a seat. This is Jonas Branford, he's one of our Lead Developers. Jonas, how are you doing? Cheers." He held up his glass and took a drink. Awkwardness hung above everyone's heads. The hostility was so outward that some of the others at the end of the table gathered their things and left.

Renata reached her hand out, "I don't believe we've met. I'm Renata Caldwell."

I reached my hand out as well, "Jonas Branford, it's great to meet you." She gave me a half-smile.

"I've heard a lot about you," I said, "Xavier tells me that your company is going to merge with Red Index and BionicShift. That's exciting! Though, I don't see Ellis Murdoch and Donovan White, here. Do you think they're running late, Xavier?"

Renata said "Oh, I didn't realize we were talking about confidential information! Yes, I suppose we are going to be merging companies. Xavier, when did you make that announcement?" Renata smiled at Xavier.

He said "Forgive him, Renata, he doesn't realize that information is confidential and could result in his termination if he doesn't keep that to himself. As far as where Ellis and Donovan are, well, Jonas, you might know better than I do." Xavier repositioned himself in his chair and slouched a bit, crossing his arms.

"Yeah, I think I do," I said, leaning forward "but I'm not sure where their bodies are. Do you know?"

Renata's expression changed and she said, "I think you better keep your mouth shut about all that." Her voice was shaky. "You don't know who you are talking to."

I turned my head to look her in the eye as she sat next to Xavier. "You'd be surprised by what I know, Renata." Her jaw clenched as her eyes scraped the back of my skull.

Xavier interrupted. "Let's calm down for a second and take a step back. He doesn't know shit, Renata."

He pointed at me, with his hand extended "You're a fucking parasite, and you must be wondering why you aren't dead yet. I must say, though, I'm surprised by your presence. How did you even get in here? Walking into my party like this, I've gotta give you credit. It's brave! Stupid as hell, but brave." He took a drink and continued, "I didn't want to do this here but looks like you ripped off that band aid. I'm not fond of violent confrontations in front of my staff and cohorts so what's it going to take to send you back out into the wild so we can hunt you down again?" He finished his drink and motioned a waiter over. "I'll take another one, and bring one for him too."

I didn't say anything and Renata spoke again, "Xavier, who the fuck is this guy? Lead Developer, my ass! What have you gotten me involved in now?"

Xavier attempted to extinguish the situation by reassuring her that I wasn't someone to be concerned with. She snapped back at him "Enough with the bullshit, tell me who this guy is before I pull out of this fucking deal!" Renata's voice was shrill and cutting through loud enough for others around us to hear. I smirked and covered my mouth to hide my smile. She had Xavier's attention and he moved his shoulder toward her. The waiter came back over and there was an awkward, weighted silence while he set the drinks on the table.

Xavier waited until the waiter was gone and said "Look, I'll handle this, let me talk it out. There's no need to get worked up." Turning his head back to me, he said "Jonas, really, what do you want? How much money will it take for you to go away?"

I shook my head and said "I'm not interested in money. I'm interested in a shift in philosophy that I don't believe you're capable of. You seem to know a lot about me, but how did you figure that out? Why don't we talk about that?"

Xavier raised his hand up in a dismissive manner and said "We're not going to get into those details. I need you to leave now, Jonas. Like I said to you the other day, I do think you're a crafty guy and I could use someone like you in my ranks. But, consider my offers rescinded, cash or otherwise. You seem like too much of a liability so I'm going to wrap this up. You were lucky to be alive and I'm afraid your luck has run out." He nodded his head over to the security guards watching nearby. They came to the table and had me flanked on both sides.

I put my hands under the table and pressed my palms into the underside. My leg bounced with anxiety. I didn't want to cause a scene. That would go against my plan. But I was about to be abducted, the game was ending. Security wasn't going to kick me out, they were going to dispose of me. 'Terminated' as Xavier had said before. And he meant it.

I stayed seated and kept talking. "Are these guys armed? Seems like a big risk to take, with all of these bystanders." I took the final sip out of my glass.

Renata slammed her hand down on the table, "Oh, shut the fuck up, you little shit! Get the hell out of here before we make you disappear!"

Xavier looked at me, "Come on, Jonas, time's up."

I put my head down and said, "yeah, I agree. Time is up".

1 6

I jumped up from my chair, took the empty glass and smashed it against the face of the guard on my left. Then I flipped the table over, kicked the other guard in his shin and slammed him into the legs. A contentious conversation had boiled over into a hectic confrontation in a matter of seconds. Renata and Xavier, caught by surprise, both stumbled to the floor. I took a gun away from one of the guards and pointed it at Renata. She was going to be my way out of this hotel. I knew I could find Xavier again and that he would come looking for me, in full force. But Renata was too slippery for me to let her get away. The rest of the party continued for a minute until someone saw that I was holding a gun. Panic spread like fire in a drought. People ran out of the ballroom, screaming. So much for not wanting to scare anyone.

I grabbed Renata by the shoulder and wrapped my arm around her neck with the gun pressed against her temple.

I looked at Xavier as he got to his feet and I said, "I'm taking her with me, and you're going to let me go. You and me… we'll hash this out later, but I'm leaving. Tell your security to stand down."

Xavier's unwavering confidence evaporated and a look of concern overcame his face. "OK, Jonas, no one's gonna stop you." He said, with his hands raised. An emergency exit had been pushed open and it set off the fire alarms. Security rushed in and found a hostage situation unfolding. I dragged Renata across the room. The music had stopped and been replaced with commotion. Xavier was next to his security and watched as I continued stepping back with Renata's neck in my grip. Her hands dug into the sleeve of my jacket. I wanted to bear the collapse that was upon us all and it felt satisfying to put fear into their hearts.

Once outside, the security had me surrounded but I maintained the upper hand. "Stay where you are, or I'll kill her!" I shouted to everyone that could hear me. Xavier told his team to stay back. Someone had dialed 911 in the midst of my takeover, and sirens could be heard not too far away. And they were moving closer. I had to get to my car as fast as possible. I took Renata back to the rooftop of the parking garage, forced her inside, and drove through the different levels. She was furious and not at all afraid. Hurling insults at me and questioning whether I was even, as she put it, "man enough" to kill her. I didn't say anything. I kept focused on fleeing the scene. I had managed to escape before the police got to the hotel and I knew Xavier would send his security after me and try to delay involvement from the authorities. He was a criminal, like the head of a cartel. No one understood the full extent of his enterprise aside from himself but there were always rumors that blurred into facts about his money laundering and drug running. Of course, the police don't care if Xavier doesn't want them to intervene. If a crime was committed, an investigation would ensue. The delay from the police chase helped me get away but that didn't concern Xavier. His security team, composed of other criminals, would take payments to search for me. The bounty on my head would be a huge payout, including drugs, hookers, or any other unsavory garbage he could provide. I had crippled his plans and embarrassed him, his ego had been steam rolled. And he couldn't have that.

"You aren't going to hurt me, young man. You're too afraid. Jail would be rough for a pretty guy like you. And the kind of connections Xavier has… shit, you'd be lucky to make it past day one. Where are we going anyway?" She asked.

I kept my eyes focused on the road in front of me. I knew where I was going and she would figure that out soon enough.

"You have to say something to me, sometime. You were awful chatty back at the party. What, you don't wanna talk to me now? If you're so brave, why not just shoot me right here?" She continued, "No, I don't think you're gonna do a damn thing to me, sweetie."

We parked outside the Fountain Research building. It had been taped off by the police but it was unoccupied.

"Let's go." I said as I yanked her out of the car by the arm. I pressed the gun into her back and we went into the lobby. I walked her over to the front desk and grabbed a pad and paper.

"I need you to write down Xavier's home address." I said.

Scoffing, she said, "I'm not giving that to you."

I said "OK, then. I guess I'll figure it out myself." I shoved her back a couple of feet and shot her twice in the head. Her body fell and that was the end of that. The smell of the gunpowder permeated as blood, and not oil, pooled on the floor. All of the extravagance that I put forth in finding her came to an unceremonious end. Just like that, she was dead.

And it turns out she was human. That was unexpected considering her lack of normal human emotions and the way she treated people. I'm sure she had been dosing MORS, or was heading that direction.

The MORS technology, as far as I understood it, had been developed alongside the living, Organic Machines. It was later on that elitist, wealthy people started to inject themselves with the technology. The hope was that it would keep their organs functioning, thus achieving an unheard-of-since-Biblical-times longevity. There was an inherent intimidation factor that accompanied the idea of "living forever". Evil politicians, or "not good" political world leaders, had no expiration date. I don't think that every world or government staffer that consumed MORS wanted to live forever with the sole purpose of continuing a reign of terror over the masses. That was more so a "perk", if anything. And the mechanical security surrounding them all was another layer of protection against a public fed up with the policies and handiwork of CyberSynth.

We would often ask ourselves "who even is CyberSynth? Who belongs to this club? Who is really running the show?" The answer wasn't a matter of who, but who is not? The welded relationship between government and big business was unbreakable. The separate creatures with multiple arms had been fused together, for the most part, and two became one. Whatever the governments around the world wanted, CyberSynth would work to implement, and whatever CyberSynth wanted, the governments would also implement. Of course, not everyone in the future was set on sacrificing their humanity to remain youthful. And not every wealthy person was considered a part of CyberSynth. Renata Caldwell was, though. Emphasis on the "was".

Lighting the building on fire crossed my mind. However, that would end up being more of a flare in the night sky than a deterrent for the investigation into who shot and killed her. Everyone knows I pulled the trigger, whatever shroud I hid behind disintegrated as soon as the bullet left the chamber, that was fine with me. I was ready to step out into the open. Before I fled the scene, I threw open every drawer in the front desk looking for information on Xavier's residence. I dug through page after page of boring, useless paperwork until I found a multi-page invoice with a "bill to" address for Xavier. It looked like his property was also being used as a storage for supplies since there were hundreds of items listed in alphabetical order. Nothing was of interest to me, other than the fact that he had enough space to store crates of supplies for Fountain Research. There must have been more to this because it did seem weird for Xavier to offer his home for storage of makeup, among other items. I flipped to the other page and saw line after line of orders for firearms, ammunition, and explosives. Xavier must have gotten himself into some trouble so he was trafficking the weapons through Fountain Research. At the bottom of the page was a handwritten note above the address:

Store in the outbuilding,
to the right of the hangar
9473 County Road 75

I took the note with me and got back in the car. Once back at the hotel, I laid my weapons on the table, magazines and all. I didn't bother counting the rounds I had left over but it should be more than enough. I loaded each magazine for the rifle, and the one I had for the 9mm. I needed to be more than prepared so I made a plan to stop at the Guns & Ammo Depot and pick up one of those ballistic vests I saw on display, another magazine for the 9mm, and any other useful supplies. Part of the plan was to explore the cache of weapons stored at Xavier's property, if I could make it that far. The next day was going to be all out war between myself and who knows how many other people.

Standing almost no chance was not enough to prevent me from following through. If anything, it was motivation to press on anyway. I had already come this far, there was no use in turning back now.

The next morning, I printed more money, loaded everything into the back seat and drove over to the gun store. I had bullets stuffed in the pockets of my pants and in my jacket and boxes on the front seat. I felt unhinged, like I had been scrawling the names of people I wanted to kill on my rifle. The edge most of us sit on when we are stressed out eroded from underneath me. I was now suspended in the air of uncertainty. Every second ticking by was years off my life.

The door to the store was propped open and it was empty on the inside, at least from the parking lot view. Inside, the same man was behind the counter, but he didn't react. He must not have remembered me. No conversations or small talk today. Right away, the vests came into view as well as another mannequin further down that had on full body protective gear. A sign was taped to the chest that read "Modular High Impact Crowd Control Suit w/Bullet Proof Vest. $799".

I called out to the clerk, "Excuse me, do you have this one in stock?"

"Yes, sir, give me a minute."

He walked off to the back and I waited by the mannequin. I looked over the entire suit and felt around. The material was rugged and sturdy. It gave me an obvious advantage. The suit covered the legs, the shoulders, and torso. It also came with a shield, helmet, and gloves. I didn't plan on using those but they were nice to have all the same. The vest also had compartments for additional ammunition.

When the clerk returned with the suit, I asked him for a 9mm magazine as well and I checked out. He placed everything into a large, plastic bag and I left the cash on the counter.

Xavier's home was thirty to forty minutes outside of town. The drive was boring at best until I had stopped to put on the Crowd Control Suit. I exited the highway and parked around the back at an out-of-business tire repair shop a mile from the destination. No one could see me from the road and I was alone with nothing but an empty dumpster and brush in front of me. As I was strapping the suit to my legs and torso, an orb appeared above the ground. It was gray and yellow, like a cloud filled with lightning. It would be menacing and overwhelming to almost anyone that saw it and didn't know what it was. But I knew. It was the proprietary technology I had stolen, or part of it. And I guess CyberSynth got it right. For once, the incoming Enlisters would catch me by surprise. My rifle was within reach in the back seat. I clicked in a magazine and propped up on the hood of my car.

The first Enlister came through the open portal and I shot him in the head. I had a good vantage point, as I leaned over the hood. That Enlister fell to the ground and another stepped out. I took that one out as well, then two more stepped out. I kept firing and soon enough, I was overrun. There must have been fifty Enlisters. And it must have been a drop off point, which made sense. CyberSynth were sending Enlisters out in lower populated areas and they would migrate from there. I picked the worst possible place to pull over. Bad timing, bad luck, or both.

I jumped in my car and drove through as many as I could. I circled back around and floored it, plowing into another large group. By that point, many of them had crawled onto the car. One of them on top had managed to tear part of the roof off. I shot it point blank and oil splattered on the windshield. Its body slid off and under the front right tire. I pressed on the brakes and the rest flew off. As I was backing up, another one pounded on the back windshield, while more of them grabbed onto my car. They had me on all sides. This was the closet I had come to being taken out. And I was starting to panic. I floored it again, sharp to the left, and sent the Enlisters flying once more and my car was spun out. I straightened the wheels and continued driving not knowing the direction I was headed. Enlisters pushed their way through the hole in the roof. I floored it again, crashing into the dumpster.

The airbags deployed, my face bounced off and dust filled the cab. I was dazed and a little dizzy. I grabbed my rifle and fired it in a rage. I shot the ones on the driver's side first and kicked the door open. I got out, turned around, and shot the ones on the top of my car. Then kept firing in all directions in front of me, even after all of the Enlisters were dead on the ground. The car was done, not drivable, totaled. I sat with my eyes closed for a second and rubbed my temples. I was bleeding on my forehead, or from the top of my head. Several cuts spread across both of my hands. I was lucky to be alive, I could have run into the brick wall of that old tire repair shop, instead of the dumpster. I didn't want to think much about that. I gathered my guns, the Continuum Resetter, and my bag and started down the road.

1 7

This area was as remote as it could get. County Road 75 had two lanes and no signs of human life. Why would someone as wealthy as Xavier live way out here? Thirty minutes must have gone by as I approached the top of a hill. Not too far in the distance, I could see a handful of structures. Looking at the map on my Continuum Resetter, it was clear that it was Xavier's home, and it looked more like a compound. A huge, tan workshop off to the right, another collection of buildings on the left, I couldn't see a house but his property was massive so it must have been located in the back. There was also a gate blocking off the front and continuing all the way around the property. It was hard to imagine anyone being let in to sell windows or roof repairs. You weren't getting in there without an invitation.

Among all of the buildings and outside of the gate was a toll-booth-style booth setup. Inside the gate was a Crow's Nest tower, like what you would see in a prison yard. I rushed over to a nearby tree, crouched down at the base and faced the property below. I stared at the tower, looking for movement, but saw nothing. I sat at the base of the tree for a few minutes to catch my breath and come up with some kind of a plan.

The world had changed a lot in the decades that had passed, but not so much the way everything looked. All of the climate disasters forecasted in the beginning of the 21st century never came to pass. Most of the world looked the same, except for the normal changes brought about by humanity. New developments, neighborhoods, cities expanding, basic stuff like that had happened. But the world pretty much looked the same outside of the major metropolitan areas. I wondered if this compound of Xavier's was still standing. It might not have even changed in all those years. I assumed it would all disappear and I would no longer exist after I killed Xavier. But time travel was a beast that could not be tamed and no one, not the inventors of the Continuum Resetter, not the Testers, nor the Developer or Users, knew what would happen if you made changes in the past. I guess I was a pioneer in that way. Blazing a trail so wide that the entire Earth would be burned as well.

I saw movement near the fence down below, someone must have noticed me. I tried my best to hold steady, taking short, deliberate breaths. The men here looked to be ex-Special Forces or some other type of military-level soldiers. These weren't career criminals given bullet proof vests to patrol the premises. I could tell from the way the men were carrying themselves. Squatted low to the ground, rifles at chest level, uniforms, helmets. The property must have been two hundred yards away or so. By now, I was sort of thankful I had been forced to leave my car behind. If I had come barreling in, I would have been given away as soon as I got to the top of the hill.

Thunder rumbled again and the wind picked up. I didn't like the idea of getting stuck in a downpour. The brush and forest on the outside of the compound was not that far away. I could sprint for that and head down. If I didn't get shot first. I sat and waited and watched and waited some more. I counted five different people lined up on the outside of the gate and one in the tower. And there was one in the booth controlling the entrance. The five around the perimeter were armed, along with the one in the tower. It was obvious based on their stances. No one hunches down on one knee with their arms raised for fun. I could not tell if the guard in the booth was armed, but it was safe to assume he was. I had to stride at least a hundred feet to be out of view of all of them. My chances of survival were much better heading through the forest but getting into the compound would be very difficult with the gate closed.

A bullet zipped past me on the left. Then another. No hesitating anymore. I had never moved so fast in my life. Bullets landed behind me and in front of me. I was zig zagging left and right. Avoiding being hit, by some sort of miracle, each stride felt like an eternity. The tree line was getting closer and closer but still seemed miles away.

I disappeared into the brush and the bullets stopped. Dead silence filled the air as the last shot bounced off a tree. Instead of waiting for too long, I got up, realized the men behind the gate couldn't see me as much as I couldn't see them and pressed forward. I made it to the property and walked along the fence line, inspecting it as I went for any kind of opening. I kept telling myself this place couldn't be all that big. After thirty minutes of stomping through the woods, I came to a cellar door. And it was unlocked. I lifted the doors and exposed the steel steps leading down. As stringent as Xavier was about control and security, I was beyond surprised that he had left this open. This must have been an afterthought since the grass had overgrown around the doors and rust had begun to set in on the edges. Either that, or it was a trap.

I picked up a rock and tossed it down the steps. I heard it bang and crash and stop not too far down. I felt cool air escaping, and comparing that with the heat of the day setting in, descending into a cave with no light source didn't seem like the worst idea.

I hesitated.

It took some self-convincing to place one foot on the steel steps. I was still armed. My Control Baton was in my bag, along with lots of bullets, a 9MM, extra magazines, and I had my rifle in my hands. To my teeth, I was armed. So I took one step, then another, and then another. Pretty soon, I was below the door line and it was well behind my back. The light from outside lit a path that didn't go very far. Pretty soon, I was out of the light and into the darkness.

1 8

I think it is human nature to have a fear of the dark. Like the fear of the unknown. A lot of people have that fear. No one enjoys being in a pitch black room alone, for that reason. We don't know who, or what, is in there. It goes against our nature to go into a place where we can't see. Our eyes are the window to the soul, sure, but our eyes are also our guides to self-preservation. No one runs into a burning building, unless you're paid to do so; or your loved ones are inside. No amateur sees a tornado and goes over to shake its hand. And no one opens a hatch leading to a dark place and walks inside, not without a flashlight, at least. Darkness is intimidating. We can't see what we can't see and that sets off all kinds of alarms in the human psyche. All living creatures have an instinct to not place themselves in the path of harm. I had stifled that instinct for most of my journey. Until now. In what must have been years, I had a genuine fear.

Fear is good for nothing, after all. It may save you from danger or death, but fear does not lead to success. Fear leads to comfort, and sometimes comfort leads to unhappiness. Fear leads to the question of "what if?" What if you hadn't been afraid to take that risk? Maybe it would have paid off? Maybe you would have died? Maybe things are better because you were afraid. But maybe things aren't better. Maybe fear made things worse. Fear is useless but still, we cannot help ourselves. We can't predict the future, but we do our best, and fear tends to be the spirit guide.

I had been standing in one spot for at least ten minutes, waiting on a metal platform in a narrow hallway. I was stuck in a singular tunnel system with one way in and one way out. My eyes had adjusted enough for me to see that everything was clean and the walls and ceiling were very close in proximity. It was two feet above my head and I could extend my arms all the way but the tips of my fingers touched the sides of the tunnel. It was a tight fit and it made me uncomfortable to the point of being claustrophobic. I kept taking deep breaths, feeling like the next one might be my last. But the air was cool, it had to be coming from an air conditioning unit. Or it could be because it was below the surface. Like how a cave is cool even in the summertime. I figured this tunnel was an emergency escape route that had been forgotten. It looked like it was built and then left alone. There were no signs of activity. No pests, no water, dripping, no smell. Just a long, concrete tunnel, leading somewhere. I had my rifle pressed against my shoulder as I crept along, though I hoped I wouldn't have to fire it down here. The sound would be enough to knock anyone off of their feet and I didn't want to think about what it would do to my hearing. My grip was tight around my gun. And my steps were slow. I was expecting someone to appear and tackle me to the ground. I kept visualizing a fatal confrontation, being captured from behind, so I kept looking back every so often to make sure no one was there. Thankfully, no one ever was.

When you're paranoid, you're never alone. There is always someone watching. Plotting to take you out. Listening in. Did you say something out loud? Someone heard it. Whatever you're thinking, someone can hear that too. Was someone already waiting on the other end? Where did this even lead? I was within Xavier's property line so it did lead somewhere and it didn't seem feasible for it to continue on for miles. Dark and cold, representative of Xavier's very nature, though I'm sure that was not intentional. He must have been so arrogant that he never considered he would have to use this escape route. And judging from the security guards ready to kill on command, each of them would die before he ever would. I didn't expect him to even take part in the fighting. I assumed he would sit back and watch as his men came at me full force, every gun blazing.

After a while, I got impatient and counted my steps. One hundred, soon after, two hundred, then three hundred. That was on top of the hundreds of steps I had already taken. The tunnel was endless. My hand was beginning to sweat and I could feel cold sweat run down my back as well. I loosened my hand and stopped walking. I had been gripping the rifle so hard that it was throbbing when I let go. I took another deep breath. I had to be reaching the end, it couldn't continue for much longer. I took another step and the muzzle of my rifle hit something. I felt around and found a smooth, horizontal handle. I turned it with a slight motion and it was unlocked. I turned it further, and light poured in. I had been going up a ramp right before I got to the door, I hadn't realized it. And it led to an empty warehouse that looked more like a hangar. The small plane added to that aesthetic. It was confusing as to why there was a plane and an escape tunnel but I guess Xavier wanted to be prepared. I heard the air conditioner in the hangar and felt the cool air billowing in from large ducts in the ceiling. Another confusing feature. Why would he need to keep this place cool all the time? It was excessive, but typical for a person with a lot of money, I supposed. I kept my gun raised but this place was empty, except for a plane and some crates.

Out of curiosity, and looking for any kind of advantage, I opened one of the crates with a crowbar laying on the top. It was filled with packing straw and a lot of guns. Most of them were hand guns or .22 rifles and things that were easier to conceal. Knives and other handheld weapons. I put the lid back on that one and moved onto another one. More guns, and bullets, but nothing too extraordinary. The same applied to the third one. I didn't understand the need to filter the guns and bullets through a purchase order with a boat load of beauty supplies. Everything was backwards. The amount of guns in there could be acquired with cash at various gun stores, or through a distributor with no issues. Everything did have a military look and feel so there was a tinge of arms smuggling in the air. But still, it was a bunch of handguns and small rifles. The fourth crate gave me a sinking feeling in my stomach as the lid hit the floor.

It was crammed with C4 explosives, detonators, hand grenades, and flash bangs. Small box after small box of very dangerous weapons. I didn't think Xavier was hoarding this for himself. I looked at the plane again and realized something. Its hatch was opened and laid right near the crates. Xavier was going to traffic these weapons and explosives. They could end up all over the world. I knew he had ties to terrorist groups in some way, but I didn't know he was involved to this level. Part of me wanted to blow everything up and another part of me wanted to run to the nearest police station. But I was a criminal too. I would get arrested and these crates and their contents would be out in the wild. Serial numbers filed, any trace tied to Xavier burned up and obfuscated. He would be a free man, meanwhile I would be taken to a mental hospital to live out my days. Telling people I was from the future, doped up on meds to keep me calm and quiet for decades.

"Fuck that." I said to myself. I took some C4 out of the crate, walked over to the plane, and strapped it to the underside using the materials it came with. The detonators had a wireless range of up to three thousand feet, according to the instructions. It was scary how simple it was to set up and arm. In the wrong hands, this amount of explosives could kill a lot of people. I put the detonator in my bag and heard the hangar door open. I ducked down behind the crates and listened. A man was pacing through, speaking over a walkie-talkie.

"I'm checking in the hangar, over." His footsteps echoed and he was getting closer.

My eyes were darting to the left and right with my back pressed against the crates. Sweat ran down my temples.

Another voice crackled over the radio, "Connor, hurry the fuck up. Xavier said he's not going to be in there, over."

Connor shot back, "I'm almost done, dick head, over."

He approached from my left so I pivoted around with my rifle aimed steady. He was not as ready for me as I was for him. He and I fired at each other. His was more "from the hip" and frightened, mine was right into his chest. The shots he fired hit the ceiling and he fell back, dead.

His radio was buzzing with the guy on the other end asking what had happened. Of course, he didn't answer, and it was not far-fetched to assume there would be reinforcements readying their weapons. I didn't want to be stuck in here next to all those explosives among a flurry of gunfire. My next obstacle was not knowing what was on the other side of that door that guy had entered through. I didn't have very long to process or decide on whether it was a good idea. It was an idea, and one that I had no choice but to go with. I stomped towards the door, with the butt of my rifle pressed firm against my shoulder. I was slow but steady, my finger rested near the trigger. I half-expected the door to fly open at any moment. And I was right.

A group of five or six security guards burst into the room and a fight broke out. One of them fell down with a shot to the head. I tried to get away, but the others managed to knock me to the floor and I dropped my gun. I was being beaten from every angle, kicked, punched, pistol whipped. They were trying to put my hands behind my back. I managed to kick someone in the knee and trip him onto the others. He fell as I crawled away and took the Control Baton out of my bag.

While I climbed to my feet, the scuffle had devolved into a staring contest. I didn't quite understand why I hadn't been killed already. I hit the extension button and waited. They were huddled together, muttering to each other. Then two of them lunged at me. I let off a full swing and their bodies were thrown back.

There were three left, standing in disbelief. "Come on, guys," I spit blood at their feet, "you can do better than that." One of them had his gun trained on my forehead. A small argument began to play out. There was a debate about the legitimacy of

Xavier's comments wanting me to remain alive. I watched the three of them as their conversation continued to heat up. One was looking at the gunman, the other was looking at the two of them, saying nothing, and the gunman was looking right at me. That was, until the conversation went sideways and he took his eyes off of me. As soon as that happened, I stepped forward, broke his hand with the Control Baton, and jabbed the other guy in the face with the top of it. The third guy came to his senses and ran in a direction I was expecting. He was into the escape tunnel before I knew it and on his way. I guess he didn't want to partake in the action any longer.

I picked up my guns, and used the shirt of one of the dead security guards to wipe the rest of the blood off of my face. The adrenaline was still lingering, but I was sore. My face hurt and I might have had a broken nose. I was glad that I had the tactical gear, otherwise, I would have to include broken ribs in my list of ailments. I pushed open the door to the hangar and looked around. I didn't see anyone and couldn't hear anything except a slight breeze. The total size of the property must have been at least a couple hundred acres. I could no longer see the fence line and there were various outbuildings and garages filled with who knows what. I felt like I did when I first arrived in 2026: I had no idea which direction to go.

Off in the distance, I could see a dirt road, leading somewhere. And since there was no obvious home nearby, it felt logical that the road ended at Xavier's door step. I headed in that direction when a military-style Jeep came barreling around the corner with a man on the back occupying a machine gun mounted on the top. It looked like something straight out of a war movie. He peered around and before I could make a move, he set his eyes on me and fired. The bullets pierced the side of the hanger. I don't know if this idiot realized what was in there, and I'd be willing to bet he had no idea what was behind that door. Otherwise, he would have thought twice.

I sprinted and ducked behind a large shed. The sloppy gunman missed me by quite a bit. The kickback must have been too strong for him to control. And these security guards might have some combat experience but overall, Xavier's employees had a low bar of expectations. This was either a desperate tactic to stop me, or it was some moron's bright idea to take the decommissioned US Military Jeep for a spin.

Once I rounded the nearest building, I could hear the engine rumbling as the driver inched closer, still in front of the hangar. And another Jeep with the same setup was approaching as well, from the opposite direction. I hid behind some barrels and I could see the Jeep closing in and heading for the hangar as well. I wasn't so sure I could escape this on foot. What if the other gunman on the second Jeep was a better shot? Luck was on my side from the moment I stole the Continuum Resetter but it was on "E". I couldn't push it any further, trying to run on foot again.

I took the detonator out of my bag and held it in my hand. I hadn't put any thought into what I would do with it, or if I was even going to push the little red button. It had seemed like a "grand finale" gesture. I would drag Xavier's body over and blow him up along with it. That idea was brief and fleeting. No, I would have to use this as my introduction. My way of letting Xavier know his day of reckoning was here. It takes a certain type of person to purchase all of those explosives and weapons, with plans to distribute them to the criminal underworld. And that is the same type of person, with almost infinite wealth, who works to develop a technology to take over and control society from near and far. And it takes another type of person to rig those explosives and set them off at once. And that same type of person goes to great lengths to put a stop to the other person's plans before the plans are even flushed out. He and I were oil and water. Better than that, we were the unstoppable force and the immovable object, colliding in midair.

I had to admit to myself that an explosion's blast radius was not my forte. And I had no idea how much explosive material was in those crates. But I needed to get as far away as I could. Further down the property stood another huge, metal garage. That was my new destination. As soon as I stepped out from behind the barrels, the driver and the gunman of the second Jeep would see me. That was almost certain. I inhaled and exhaled, put my gun over my shoulder with the strap and put my bag on my other shoulder. Gripping the detonator in my hand, I stood up and looked at the gunman, who had been talking with the driver of the other Jeep. He looked at me, pointed, and the two Jeeps sped toward me, sending a cloud of dirt in the air. I ran in a zigzag pattern to avoid being hit. And instead of heading for the other building, I took a sharp left. My plan had fallen apart and so I devised a new one without much thought. I dove off to the side, hit the dirt, and pushed the button on the detonator.

1 9

The explosion sent the Jeeps spinning out of control. One of them rolled, the other crashed into a wall and smoke filled the air. It was a thousand degrees with bits of metal raining down from above. No more stealth, no more sneaking around.

Full tilt.

I pressed my finger down on the trigger. The drivers of both Jeeps got out and fired back. The two gunmen had been thrown and were out of the picture. I bolted and was met by yet another group of security guards. I fired at them as well and hit some but didn't stay for long. Xavier had to be here somewhere. I kicked open a random door and was surprised by what I saw. Rows and rows of Enlister prototypes filled the warehouse. Each of them were stripped down and looked to have pre-dated my tenure at CyberSynth. I couldn't believe it. I slammed the door shut and pretended like I hadn't seen anything. Too many other things were happening at once and I didn't have the mental space to process a room full of dangerous, albeit deactivated, Organic Machines. I saw another wave of armed guards charging my way. At least fifty of them, almost identical, eerie looking with dark eyes, and automatic weapons. Running full speed, like a gang of brainwashed, perfect soldiers. I guess Xavier decided to push all of his chips onto the proverbial table.

His compound was crumbling and panic was in the air. An insidious effort on my part, I had managed to seep in through the cracks and everything was breaking. I wanted to be a wrench in the apparatus and it was a success. But it wasn't over yet. I shot one in the head and as it fell, oil splattered and the clan remained unfazed. I kept firing, knocking down more, before I had to run again.

As bullets zipped by, I had been hit in the back and kept getting knocked over. Smoke from the fire continued to fill the air. I found a place to hide so I reloaded my magazines and tried to catch my breath. This was an all out war zone and I knew this was it for me. The curtain above the stage was beginning to fall. I had to make a final push to find Xavier. In my bag, I still had boxes of bullets. Not too far out in front of me was a water tower with a ladder. While the group of Organic Machines wandered around and searched for me, I scaled the ladder and ducked down next to the tower. I had an excellent vantage point and unloaded as many rounds as possible into the crowd below. And they fired back. I took hits to my chest, and got knocked back into the water tower. No space for pain, I sat back up and fired more rounds. Bullets ricocheted off of the water tower. Soon after, water started to spill out.

As the water gushed down, the Organic Machines that had gotten wet were failing. Their one weakness had always been water. The organic material their skin was made from was not impervious to fluids and their AI operating system could not keep up with the speed of rushing water. I stopped firing at the crowd and turned my attention toward the tower. I fired shots at an existing hole above my head. And as soon as a handful of Organic Machines had made it to the top of the ladder, the tower burst. Sending everyone down to the ground, including me.

I landed on the ground with the wind knocked out of me. I crawled away to try to get to dry land. I did not want to be caught in the electrified puddles as the Organic Machines dropped and shorted out. The ones that I had shot were like cut cords still plugged into an outlet. Sparks flew and water continued spraying out of the tower. I laid on the ground and looked up at the black sky. I rolled onto my side and sat up.

Everything was silent, other than the water hitting the ground. I was sore all over my body, I had cuts on my hands, my clothing was ripped, my mouth was bleeding. My eyes swelled. The fall had taken a lot out of me. But I was still searching for Xavier.

My better judgment, my instincts, told me to head down that dirt road I had noticed earlier. I shot the remaining Organic Machines that were reaching for my feet. The trail was in the opposite direction and as I carried on, I knew that I was alone. At least in this part of the property. The security guards that were human had all been killed. I didn't remember shooting all of them but I emptied the clip of my rifle over and over. At one point, my body was moving faster than my mind could keep up. The Organic Machines had been wiped out as well. And to prevent any surprises, I went back to the warehouse with the stripped down Organic Machines, stood in the doorway and unloaded another magazine.

Afterwards, I walked over to the burning building, grabbed a piece of wood that was on fire, and tossed it into the warehouse. I repeated that with everything around me that would burn. I wanted nothing to be left standing. Once I had gotten to the dirt road, every separate structure was on fire, and the flames grew higher and higher.

Then, a garage door opened. As the fire devoured the building, a man came running out. It was the guy that I thought had fled through the tunnel. I followed him with my eyes as he ran off. I didn't know what to make of what was happening but it didn't take long for things to materialize. With the garage engulfed, I saw someone else standing there. He was untouched even though he was standing in the middle of it all. His head was down, all I could see was a black hood and the outline of his body. He looked up at me and I knew what was next.

20

The Super Enlister stepped out into the open. His metal arms shimmered in the light. His expressionless face was even more terrifying than I remembered. I wasted no time shooting the guy who set him free in the back. I thought he was someone who had fled for reasons of conscience. In reality, he was the king of all cheap shots. I turned my gun and fired at the Super Enlister. He walked toward me as his body absorbed every bullet. It was like shooting into a lake. His skin rippled then returned to normal. My gun was useless.

His pace was steady so I tried to run. As soon as I turned my back, he jumped forward with his shoulder and knocked me to the ground. Then he picked me up by my shirt and threw me into an empty barrel. I fumbled with my bag while gasping for air. I lifted my 9mm and shot him in the face. He slapped it out of my hand and I tried to crawl away but he grabbed my foot and threw me again. My rifle landed out of reach and that didn't matter anyway. I laid on my stomach and coughed. It was over for me. My body was giving up, my mind was tattered, this was the end. As he stomped over toward me, I accepted that I was done. He lifted me up and punched me in the face. As he dropped me onto the ground, my head was spinning. The Super Enlister's stomach hatch opened and he pulled out a set of handcuffs attached to shackles. I kept my eyes on him and he walked over to me. He held out the cuffs and went to grab my wrist.

"Enlister, command initialize." I said as I pulled the Control Baton out of my bag.

He stopped and his eyes shifted to purple "Go ahead, sir."

"Wow, I didn't think that would work." I said as I pressed the extension button and hit him in the forearm, splitting it down the middle. "I didn't think that would work, either."

He stumbled back and tried to charge toward me, but I swiped him across the face. His jaw was ripped off and the skin around his skeleton went with it. I hit him again on the opposite side of the face. His body shuddered as he fell to his knees. I hit him again across the top of his head. Then again in the back. And on an up-swing, I hit his jaw and he fell back. I knelt down with my foot over his chest and jammed the top of the Control Baton into his mouth where it stayed.

What was left of him locked up and started to shake. I heard a whining noise as he vibrated faster and faster. I backed up at first then ran off once I realized what was about to happen. Before long, the Super Enlister exploded, sending parts of his body everywhere. The irony of the moment didn't disappoint. I laughed to myself, reloaded my magazines and headed to find Xavier's house.

The dirt road I started down was long. There were deep grooves with grass growing in between and the tire tracks appeared fresh. It had to lead somewhere. It was open all around with no trees close to the road. This part of the property looked to have been landscaped by a professional as it was well maintained and beautiful. There were small hills and the winding road led through a pasture of lush green grass and wildflowers; with a small pond off to one side. It looked like it was right out of a nature magazine. I couldn't believe that someone so evil lived there.

I continued down the road and around a bend. From there, I could see Xavier's mansion with a single car in the front. I couldn't tell if anyone else was there but I was prepared for another fight. Even if I had felt like I had been run over by a truck.

There was a fountain in the middle of a circle drive made out of cobblestone. And a swarm of dragonflies hovered around the water. It was the most amazing group of insects I had ever seen in my life. Purple, green, red, orange, blue, so many colors were fluttering around. I was mesmerized. Even after everything I had been through, I was still captivated by nature and its beauty.

One of the dragonflies landed on the barrel of my rifle and I lifted the gun up to examine it. It was blue with clear, gray wings, and massive eyes. Its legs moved in an almost mechanical way as it crawled along the tip of my rifle. So mechanical that it looked fake. I put out my finger and it climbed up. I brought it closer and rotated my finger to see all around it. It turned its head and made a whirring sound like a camera refocusing. I grabbed it with my other hand and snapped it half. Not to my surprise, oil and wires were exposed. Every one of these magnificent insects in front of me were Drones. Decorative Drones, on display at the fountain as a way for Xavier to showcase his extravagance and technological advancements. I'm sure every guest he had marveled at his creation. I took my bag off my shoulder and swung it around in a fury as hard as I could. Everything about him was fabricated, artificial, nothing was genuine, except for how vile he was. He had people killed, he was an elitist, he felt like he was better than the rest of us. So much better that he created machines to control us all.

I went around the fountain, up to his vehicle, and held down the trigger. I blasted out the glass, the tires, and continued onto the front of his home. I stopped and heard the last shell casing hit the ground.

I shouted at the top of my lungs, "Xavier!"

I waited and he spoke through a speaker on one of the columns on the front porch. "Come on around back, Jonas. I've been expecting you."

He was sitting on his patio at a round table, with two empty glasses and a bottle of liquor. His backyard looked like a resort. There were cabanas and a full bar. Along with a massive pool and another fountain. He poured the liquor into both glasses.

"Here you go, Jonas. Have a drink. You look like you've been through Hell." He lifted his glass, took a drink, then poured himself another. "I did not think you would make it this far. But here you are. I have to admit, you have been nothing but a bad dream since I first figured out who you were. Even though I don't know much about you. So, tell me about yourself."

I stared at him with my hand on my rifle. "Come on, Jonas. Don't give me that stone cold silent bullshit. I've got a guy with a sniper rifle pointed right at your head. So as soon as I lift my left hand, you're going to die." He pointed with his right hand above his left shoulder and sure enough, there was someone sitting up there on the second story pointing a gun at me.

"So again, tell me about yourself!" He shouted.

"Xavier, I think you already know." I said.

He replied "Yeah, but I want to hear you say it. Tell me, Jonas, where are you from?! Remember, death is almost here so make this count!"

I looked back up at the sniper and smiled. "I'm from the future. I stole a technology that I helped design, while working for your company. The company that you were planning on forming until I showed up here."

He laughed and said "There it is! I am astonished that you managed to pull that off. I don't know anything about the future, but I know about what kind of technology I have at my disposal now and I can only imagine how tough it must have been for you to get your hands on a device that would send you back. It's un-fucking-believable! To be honest, I'm looking forward to what the future has in store for me and my company. You do know that I'm going to put everything back together don't you? You can't escape my grasp, Jonas. You think you're going to stop me?" He laughed. "Jonas, you can't stop me. I've got plans bigger than you'll ever be. Or, I should say, ever were."

His left elbow lifted off the table as he put his hand up. I dashed out of the way as fast as I could. The sniper fired but he missed. Instead, I lifted my rifle and shot him. He fell from the window and crashed into the ground below.

Xavier lifted his glass and took another drink.

"Now, I can't say that I was expecting that. What is it that you want Jonas? Do you want money? Women? What? What do you want?!" He shouted.

I lifted my rifle and pointed it at him and said "I think you know what I want, Xavier." Out of nowhere, police cars came screeching through the grass.

"Drop your weapon and put your hands on your head!" A voice demanded over a loud speaker. Several police officers surrounded me, exiting their vehicles and lining up, ready to shoot.

"I said, drop your weapon and put your hands up!" The officer repeated.

Xavier put his hands up and said he was unarmed. He was playing the victim and doing a great job at that. He told them that I had taken him hostage. It couldn't end this way. He had to die and I wasn't going to be taken down until he had a bullet in his head.

The officer spoke again "Put your weapon down now or we will have to use force. This is your last warning!"

In the midst of all of the chaos, it had never occurred to me that the commotion would draw the attention of the neighbors. Someone must have called 911. I could now hear fire trucks and ambulances, a barrage of emergency vehicles descended on the property.

I titled my head with my eyes still locked on Xavier.

"Yeah, I'm sorry, but I'm not gonna do that."

I pulled the trigger of my rifle and hit him right in the forehead. As his body fell to the ground, the police converged on me. Everything went black when a bullet hit the back of my skull. I was certain that I was dead. The sound began fading and I could hear muffled shouting. I was on my side and saw blood pouring out of Xavier's face as he laid on the concrete. He was no longer breathing, he was dead. I was dead too but it didn't matter, I closed my eyes and faded away.

All of a sudden, I saw a bright flash of light and a loud noise filled my ears. I opened my eyes and was in a place I had never been before. Everything was well organized and clean. I was in the living room of a home, on a sunny afternoon. I saw a picture of myself with a group of people on the mantle. I took it off the mantle and held it. There was a large group of people seated at a table in a restaurant. Clint and Ramsey were there as well.

I held onto the picture and walked around the home. Everything was familiar but I couldn't figure out why. The smell, the feeling the house gave me, all were like deja vu. In the master bedroom, I saw a computer sitting at a desk. A screensaver with the date was spinning on the screen. It read "June 30th, 2076." I took a step back and gasped. I splashed water on my face in the bathroom. Could this be real? Did I survive? From the other room, I could hear a ringing sound. The Continuum Resetter sat on a dresser. I picked it up and saw "Call From Mom" displayed on the screen. My hand was shaking as I answered.

"Hello?" I said, not sure who was on the other end.

My mother responded "Hey, honey, are you and Lenore and the kids still coming over for dinner tonight?"

Without even thinking I said "Yeah, she'll be home in a little while and we'll head over after that."

My mom replied, "OK, that sounds good. We'll see y'all in a bit! Love you."

I said "Love you too," and hung up the phone. Lenore was my wife, we met when I was in my late twenties, we had been together for eight years. We had three children together. My mind was inundated with memories from separate timelines. My wedding, the birth of my children, and my time in 2026. It was all there. I picked up the Continuum Resetter. It had changed from before. The Distancing program was gone and it looked more like a handheld computer than anything else. But the recordings and data I collected were still available.

I rushed back into the bedroom and sat down at my desk. I entered the password I didn't realize I knew, opened a notepad program, and began typing: It's difficult to remember which year I traveled back from. Was it 2080 or 2075 or maybe 2070? I don't know. The Time Keeper on my Continuum Resetter broke when I went back.